"I know wh[ ] or should not do."

Luis continued huskily, "And I do not think my soul will be eternally damned for holding you in my arms."

Caroline stiffened, but her resistance melted when his strong hands slid up from her waist....

"This—I should not do," he muttered, "but I have to." And his mouth sought the trembling sweetness of hers.

"Please, just go away, don't say anything," she pleaded when he released her.

"No? We just ignore it, is that it?" His face twisted. "Of course, I almost forgot. You are a liberated English girl. You must be used to men making love to you. It means nothing to you!"

Caroline couldn't answer. If she was destroying any lingering feeling he might have had for her, it was all for the best....

ANNE MATHER
is also the author of these

Harlequin Presents

and these

Harlequin Romances

Many of these titles are available at your local bookseller.

For a free catalogue listing all available Harlequin Romances
and Harlequin Presents, send your name and address to:

HARLEQUIN READER SERVICE,
M.P.O. Box 707, Niagara Falls, NY 14302
Canadian address: Stratford, Ontario N5A 6W2

ANNE MATHER

forbidden flame

Harlequin Books

TORONTO • LONDON • LOS ANGELES • AMSTERDAM
SYDNEY • HAMBURG • PARIS • STOCKHOLM • ATHENS • TOKYO

Harlequin Presents edition published June 1981
ISBN 0-373-10436-7

Original hardcover edition published in 1981
by Mills & Boon Limited

CHAPTER ONE

PEERING through the fly-spotted window of the hotel in Las Estadas, Caroline thought she must have been slightly mad to agree to come here. Whatever had possessed her to apply for this appointment? Why on earth had she imagined it would be exciting, a challenge, something to divert her from the sudden emptiness of her life in England? What did she, a university graduate, with honors in English and history, know of teaching an eight-year-old child, and why had she been chosen when there had obviously been others more suitable?

Of course the advertisement she had read would have interested anyone with a spark of adventure in his blood. The chance to work in Mexico—the land of the Aztecs, steeped in history and peopled by the descendants of Montezuma and Cortes. But Caroline wondered now how many of those other applicants had balked when they discovered they were expected to travel to a remote village north of Yucatan. She had spoken with several of the other girls waiting in the drawing room of the hotel suite in London, and almost all of them were of the opinion that they were to work in Mexico City.

But even when Caroline had learned where the job was she had not been discouraged. She knew a little about Mexico, or so she had imagined, and the idea of living within driving distance of the Mayan city of Chichén Itzá had been a glowing inducement. Only now, waiting in the seedy surroundings of the Hotel Hermosa—a misnomer, surely—did the full realization occur to her of what she had committed herself to, and if there had been some way she could return to Mérida without anyone's knowledge, she would have surely done so.

Outside a drenching downpour had turned the street into a muddy river and given a gray aspect to buildings already dirt-daubed and ramshackle. This was not the Mexico she had imagined, the colorful blending of past and present in a kaleidoscope of rich mosaics and even richer architecture. This was poverty and squalor, and the simple struggle for survival against enormous odds. Las Estadas had not yet felt the impact of the oil boom that was supposedly going to transform Mexico's economy. Here life was still held cheaply, governed by the whims of weather and a seemingly unkind fate. To Caroline, used to the social and cultural advantages of English society, the sight of so much deprivation was doubly shocking, and she was uncomfortably aware that she would have much preferred not to have seen what she had.

Turning away from the window, she viewed the sordid little room behind her without liking. A rag mat beside the narrow iron-railed bedspread was all the covering the floor possessed, and the water in the chipped jug on the washstand was the graveyard for the assortment of insects that had drowned there during the night. The bed itself had been lumpy and not particularly clean, but the night before Caroline had been so tired she felt she could have slept on the floor. This morning, however, she had experienced a shudder of revulsion when she saw the grubby sheets in daylight. The breakfast of hot tortillas and strong-smelling coffee still stood on the rickety table where the obsequious hotel proprietor had left it.

A knock at her door brought an automatic stiffening of her spine as she straightened away from the window to stand rather apprehensively in the middle of the floor. "Who is it?" she called, clasping her slim fingers tightly together, and then mentally sagged again when Señor Allende put his head around the door.

"*El desayuno, señorita*—it was okay?"

The hotel proprietor was enormously fat, and as he eased his way into the room Caroline couldn't help wondering how many of those people she had seen could have lived on what he ate. His girth was disgusting, and he brought with him an odor of sweat and sour tequila that caused her empty stomach to heave.

"Ah—but you have not eaten!" he exclaimed now, observing the untouched tray. "It is not to your liking, *señorita*? You want I should have Maria make you something else?"

"Thank you, no." Caroline shook her head firmly. "I, er, I'm not hungry. Could you tell me again, what time did Señor Montejo say he would be here?"

"Don Estaban say he will come before noon," responded the fat little Mexican thoughtfully, stroking his black mustache—and viewing Caroline's slim figure with an irritatingly speculative eye. "*Mas, por cierto, el tiempo*—the weather, you understand? It may cause—how you say—the delay, no?"

Caroline's spirits sank even lower. "You mean—the roads may be impassable?" she suggested.

Señor Allende nodded. "Is possible," he agreed. Then he smiled, revealing tobacco-stained teeth. "*Mas*, no worry, *señorita*. José—" he pointed to himself "—José take good care of you till Don Estaban come."

"Yes."

Caroline forced a faint smile of acknowledgment, but she was not enthusiastic. She would not welcome having to spend another night between those dubious sheets, and Señor Allende's attitude grew increasingly proprietory. He was looking at her now as if he had some prior claim to her loyalties, while she felt she would have preferred any other hotel to this. But Señor Montejo had made the arrangements and she could only assume that this was the best Las Estadas had to offer.

"So...." Señor Allende drew a fat cigar out of his waistcoat pocket, bit off the end and spat it repulsively onto the floor. "Why do you not come downstairs and wait in my office, no? I have a little bottle of something there to—how do you say it—make the day sunny, hmm?"

He pronounced "little" as "leetle", and it was all Caroline could do not to grimace outright. Did he really imagine she might find his company appealing? If she had not felt so absurdly vulnerable she could have laughed at the predictability of it all. As it was, she took a backward step and shook her head politely but firmly.

"I don't think so, thank you," she replied crisply. "I'll stay here. I can watch the street from my window, and I wouldn't want to put you to any trouble."

"Is no trouble," exclaimed Señor Allende, spreading his hands in typically Latin fashion. "Come." He stretched out one pudgy hand. "Is much nicer downstairs."

"No!" Caroline was very definite this time. "Please—I prefer to be alone. If you'll excuse me...."

Señor Allende shrugged, and then his small eyes narrowed between the folds of flesh. "Okay, okay, is no big deal," he retorted. "*Como quiera usted!*" And with another shrug of his shoulders he left her, closing the door heavily behind him.

Caroline ran a relieved hand over the crown of her head and down to her nape, resting her head back against the support, expelling the tension that briefly gripped her. The last thing she needed was complications of that sort, and she let her shoulders droop as she walked wearily back to the window. Where was Señor Montejo? Surely a night's rain was not sufficient to cut all communications!

Pressing her palms together, she put her thumbs against her lips and gazed thoughtfully down at the veranda opposite. For the first time she questioned her own expectations of her destination. What would the Montejo house be like? What would Señor Montejo be like? And how could she have been foolish enough to commit herself to a whole month's probation when she might conceivably want to leave after only one day?

Somehow things had seemed so different in London. No one meeting Señora Garcia, who had conducted the interviews, could have had any doubts that anyone associated with her—and she was the child's grandmother—could live in anything other than exemplary surroundings. She had exuded an aura of wealth and sophistication, in keeping with the Dior suit and Cartier pearls she was wearing, and Caroline had naturally assumed her son-in-law and his daughter would be the same. Perhaps she was wrong. Perhaps Señora Garcia's daughter had married beneath her. Perhaps Señor Montejo would turn out to be more like Señor Allende....

At noon the buxom cook, Maria, brought her a bowl of greasy stew and some corn bread. Caroline suffered herself to eat a little of the stew and all of the bread, realizing it would be foolish to starve herself in this climate, and then returned to her seat by the window, wondering idly if the road to Mérida was still open.

The afternoon dragged on, and Caroline grew increasingly anxious. What if, as seemed likely, Señor Montejo did not come? How many days might she be expected to stay in this awful place?

Her eyes wandered restlessly up and down the street, watching the struggle an ancient truck was having trying to gain purchase on the slippery road, silently sympathizing as its churning wheels threw a shower of mud over an elderly woman passing by. An ox cart made better progress, though the rain was no less heavy, but her eyes were drawn to the window opposite by the waving of a cloth. She blinked when she saw that the man was trying to attract her attention, and turned disgustedly away just as the door to her room burst open.

It was late afternoon and the low-hanging clouds had left the room in partial shadow, but the hotel proprietor's bulk was unmistakable. He stood swaying on the threshold, an opened bottle of tequila clutched in his hand, and she had no need to wonder how he had spent the day.

"*¡Hola, señorita!*" he greeted her unsteadily, raising the bottle to his mouth and taking a greedy swallow. "Perhaps you like José's com—company now, hmm? You share a little drink with José, *sí*?"

Caroline knew she mustn't panic. She was not exactly afraid, but she was alarmed, and although she felt reasonably capable of defending herself should the need arise, she dreaded to think where she might go if he threw her out.

"I don't drink, Señor Allende," she said now, facing him bravely. At five feet six inches, she was almost half a head taller than he was, and infinitely fitter if his size was anything to go by.

"Do—don't drink!" he echoed, stumbling a little over his words. "*Por cierto*, you take a little tequila. Tequila is good, very good. You try some—here—here—"

He came toward her heavily, holding out the bottle, urging her to take a mouthful. Caroline's stomach lurched as she stepped aside. The idea of putting her lips where his greasy mouth had been caused the lumpy stew to rise into the back of her throat like bile, and she swallowed it back nauseously, shifting to avoid his reaching fingers.

"Señor Allende, please! I don't want to try any," she protested, moving around the bed. But he only came after her, like some lumbering buffalo, panting as his thoughts accelerated beyond the pursuit.

"You try, you try," he said over and over again, licking his lips in anticipation, and Caroline realized it was going to be impossible to get out of this without a struggle.

She was backed into a corner of the room, with the bed on one side and the wall of the room, with its tiny crucifix, on the other. Her eyes turned despairingly from the religious deity. No immortal being could help her now. With sudden inspiration she sprang onto the bed, blessing her corded jeans, which provided no swirl-ing skirts for the man to grasp. But the proprietor was more agile than she had thought, or perhaps desperation lent him speed. Whatever the truth of the matter, his plump fingers reached surely for her ankle and his brutal jerk brought her down on the bed, the unyielding mattress almost knocking the breath from her body.

In those first stunned moments she felt him clamber-ing onto the bed beside her, and now she really did panic. With a strength she hardly knew she possessed, she twisted onto her back, drawing up her knee in one swift motion, bringing it to the fleshy underside of his body with purposeful effect. His agonized groan was audible as she scrambled out from beneath him, reaching the door just as another man was about to enter. She collided helplessly with his hard body, and he had to grasp her shoulders to save himself. In the grip of panic Caroline had no thought to his identity, imagining this might be some colleague of Señor Allende come to join the fun, but as she lifted her foot to deliver a similar blow he swung her around, imprisoning her arms by her side.

"*¡Basta, basta!*" he exclaimed half angrily, and then lifted his eyes to the figure just endeavoring to climb off the bed. With Caroline still struggling in his arms he stared grimly at the obese hotel proprietor, and then, speaking in English for her benefit, he said, "What has been going on here, Allende? Did you get a little more than you had expected?"

The cultured voice, accented though it was, brought Caroline to her senses. His words, and the contemp-tuous way he said them, made her instantly aware that this was no coarse drinking partner of the sweating little proprietor. Even without Señor Allende's air of sub-dued discomfort she would have known that this was someone to be reckoned with, and her struggles stilled as he politely released her.

"I—I'm sorry if I hurt you—" she began, turning with some gratitude to her rescuer, and then her speech died away beneath the hooded gray eyes of the man confronting her.

Señor Montejo, if it was indeed he, was like nothing she had imagined. He was younger for one thing, certainly no more than thirty, and taller than most of the men she had seen since she'd arrived in Mexico. He was very dark, dark haired and olive skinned, but his features possessed all the unconscious hauteur of his Spanish forbears. He was not handsome in the accepted sense of the word. His brows were too strongly marked, his cheekbones too severe, his mouth too thin—but he was devastatingly attractive, and the moleskin jacket and pants he was wearing, over a darker brown fine wool shirt, hugged his wide shoulders and muscular thighs like a second skin. Caroline had never met anyone who exuded such an aura of raw masculinity, and for a moment she faltered, at once confused and embarrassed.

"*Señor, señor*—" Taking advantage of Caroline's discomfort, the hotel proprietor was attempting to defend himself. "You misunderstand, *señor*—"

"I think not." Señor Montejo's voice was deep and attractive. "I find you, Allende, in a position of some...shall we say, discomfort, on Señorita Leyton's bed, and the *señorita* herself, evidently in some distress—"

"Unnecessarily, I assure you, *señor*!" protested Senor Allende dramatically. "I have—I admit it—had a little too much to drink." He shrugged expressively. "So I rest for *un momento* on the *señorita*'s bed. *Que he hecho?*"

"What were you doing in the *señorita*'s room?" inquired Montejo pleasantly, but Caroline could hear the underlying core of steel in his voice.

"Perhaps—it was a misunderstanding," she murmured unhappily, unwilling to make enemies within twenty-four hours of her arrival. "I—I don't think Señor Allende meant any harm...."

Montejo's dark face assumed an ironic expression.

"Do you not?" He tilted his head in Allende's direction. "You are fortunate that Miss Leyton is not vindictive, my friend. I do not think my brother would be so generous."

Señor Allende spread his hands. "You will not tell Don Esteban, *señor*. This posada is all I have—"

The man made an indifferent gesture and said something else in his own language, but Caroline was not paying any attention. Something else, something Señor Allende had said, caused her to revise her first opinion, and she realized with sudden perception that this man was not her employer. Yet he knew her name and he had mentioned his brother. But who was he? Señora Garcia had mentioned no brother. Only that her son-in-law was a widower, living alone with his daughter and an elderly aunt on the family's estates at San Luis de Merced.

As if becoming aware of her doubts and confusion, the man turned back to her now, performing a slight bow and saying politely; "Forgive me, Miss Leyton. I have not introduced myself. My name is Montejo, Luis Vincente de Montejo, brother to Don Esteban and uncle to your charge, Doña Emilia."

"I see." Caroline gathered herself quickly. "You are—you are here to meet me?"

"Of course." Long dark lashes narrowed the steel-gray eyes. "My brother is...indisposed. He asked me to bring you to San Luis."

Caroline drew a somewhat unsteady breath and nodded. "I'll get my things."

"Permit me."

He was there before her, hefting her two cases effortlessly, indicating she should precede him from the room. The fat little hotel proprietor watched them with a mixture of relief and brooding resentment. Caroline, meeting his cold gaze, shivered. In spite of the ingratiating smile he immediately adopted she would not trust him an inch, and she hoped she never had to throw herself on his mercy.

Downstairs a group of men were gathered in the hall,

and from their attitude Caroline suspected they had
been hoping for a fight. She guessed they had known
what Allende was up to, and as they stepped back with
evident respect to let them pass, she felt an increasing
surge of gratitude toward Señor Montejo. Without his
intervention she could have expected no help from this
quarter. She pressed her arms tightly against her sides to
avoid any kind of contact.

Outside the downpour had eased somewhat, but it
was still raining. Water drained in douches from the
eaves above their heads as they crossed the muddy street
to where a scarcely identifiable Range Rover was
parked, and the shoulders of Caroline's shirt felt damp
as she scrambled with more haste than elegance into the
front seat. Her companion thrust her cases into the back
and then came around the vehicle to get in beside her,
removing his jacket as he did so and tossing it into the
back along with her luggage.

He didn't say anything as he inserted the key into the
ignition and started the engine, and Caroline endeavored
to recover her composure. It wasn't easy, with the
memory of what had almost happened still sharply
etched in her mind, but as her breathing slowed she
managed to regain some kind of perspective. In retro-
spect it seemed almost ludicrous to imagine herself
tumbling across the bed, but at the time she had known
definite fear.

"A baptism of fire, would you say?" Señor Montejo
inquired as the vehicle reached the end of the village street. Caroline glanced sideways at him. Ahead
was only jungle, vine infested and menacing in the
fading gray light, and although Las Estadas was
scarcely civilized compared to what was beyond, the
lights of the village seemed infinitely comforting.
What more did she know of this man, after all, she
pondered. Only what he had told her. And Señor
Allende's behavior, which had spoken of fear as well as
respect. But fear of what, and of whom, she had yet to
find out.

"How—how far is it to San Luis de Merced?" she ventured, not answering him.

His mouth drew down at the corners. "Not far," he replied evenly. "Between twenty and twenty-five miles. Why?" He was perceptive. "Are you afraid you cannot trust me, either?"

Caroline moistened her lips. "Can I?"

He inclined his head. "Of a surety, *señorita*." He paused. "Believe me, you have nothing to fear from me."

IT WAS DARK long before they reached their destination. The night had come quickly, shrouding the surrounding trees in a cloak of shadows, hiding the primitive landscape, concealing the sparse settlements, much like Las Estadas, if not in size then certainly in appearance. Caroline wondered how these people lived in such conditions, where they worked, how they supported themselves, what kind of education their children had. There seemed such a gulf between the man beside her and these poor peasants, but she was loathe to voice it when he did not.

The road did improve for some distance when they joined an interstate highway, but after a while they left it again to bounce heavily along a rutted track, liberally dotted with potholes. Caroline gripped her seat very tightly to prevent herself from being thrown against the man beside her, and she felt, rather than saw, him look her way.

"Are you regretting coming, *señorita*?" he inquired, again surprising her by his perception. "Do not be discouraged by the weather. It is not always like this. Tomorrow the sun will shine and you will see beauty as well as ugliness."

Caroline turned her head. "You admit—there is ugliness?"

"There is ugliness everywhere, *señorita*," he replied flatly. "All I am saying is, do not judge my country by its weaknesses. If you look for strength, you will find it."

Caroline hesitated. "That's a very profound view."

"Profundity is as easy for a stupid man to mouth as a learned one," he remarked, and she saw him smile in the illumination from the dashboard in front of him. "Do not be misled by my enthusiasm. I love my country, that is all."

Caroline was intrigued, as much by the man as by what he had said. He was a very attractive man, but she had known that as soon as she had seen him. What she had not known then was that he had a sense of humor, or that she would find his conversation so stimulating.

"Your brother," she said thoughtfully, "he runs a ranch, doesn't he? Do you work with him?"

There was a moment's silence before he answered her, and then he said, "Here we call it a hacienda. And yes, Estaban is the hacendado. But he does not run the ranch. He has a—how do you call it—an overseer to run the spread for him."

"And what do you grow? Corn? Maize?"

"Cattle," responded Montejo dryly. "My brother employs many gauchos. It is a very large holding."

Caroline nodded. She had known this. Señora Garcia had told her. And about her granddaughter, Emilia. . . .

"Your niece," she tendered now. "She's an only child, I believe."

Again there was a pause before he replied. "Yes," he said at last. "Emilia has no brothers or sisters. Her mother died when she was born."

"Oh!" Señora Garcia had not told her this. "How distressing for your brother. He must have been very upset."

"Yes."

It was an acknowledgment, no more, and Caroline found herself wondering whether she was mistaken in thinking his tone was clipped. Surely there was no suggestion that Don Esteban was uncaring of his wife's death. Surely Señora Garcia would have warned her if this was so.

Yet, she realized, she really knew nothing of these

people beyond what they chose to tell her. That was why her own parents had been opposed to her traveling so far on such a slender recommendation. If they had not felt equally strongly about her relationship with Andrew Lovell she knew they would have done their utmost to make her change her mind. As it was, they were torn in conflicting directions.

"So, you are young to have come so far alone," Montejo remarked, unconsciously interpreting her silence. "But then," he continued, an ironic twist to his lips, "English girls are more emancipated than Spanish women. They do not have restrictions put upon them as our women do."

Caroline struggled to recover her earlier enthusiasm. "Do you disapprove, *señor*?" she ventured, forcing a light tone, and waited with some misgivings for his answer.

"It is not my concern," he responded, moving his shoulders in a gesture of dismissal.

Caroline knew a moment's impatience. "You must have an opinion," she insisted, curious to know his feelings.

With a rueful grimace he avoided a pothole before replying. "Let us say I have the usual chauvinist attitudes," he remarked. "A woman is not a man, and she should not try to emulate one."

"You think that's what I'm trying to do?" exclaimed Caroline indignantly.

His laughter was low and attractive. "No one could mistake your sex, *señorita*," he assured her dryly, and she felt a not unpleasant stirring of her senses. "All I am saying is that a woman's role is not naturally that of the hunter, but that the inevitable conclusion of any continued adaptation is transformation."

Caroline gazed ahead of her, watching the headlights of the Range Rover as they searched out a marsh cactus, glimpsing, as if in a shadowy reflection, a four-legged creature moving out there in the darkness. His answer had been predictable and yet more logical than some she had heard. But it was not flattering to find oneself compared, however indirectly, to a member of the opposite sex, and she wished she had some clever response to flatten his biased argument.

"I have offended you, I think," he commented now, his tone lacking its earlier mockery. "I am sorry. I did not mean to do so. But you asked for my opinion and I gave it."

Caroline shrugged. "You haven't offended me," she declared, although, without her realizing it her whole demeanor suggested that he had. "I was trying to think of a suitable answer, that's all."

"I think you mean, a suitable setdown," he observed, giving her a wry grin. "I am sorry, truly. Believe me, you are a very feminine lady, and I salute your courage in pursuing your career."

"You don't really." Caroline would not be deceived. "You're probably one of those men who think a woman shouldn't have a brain in her head!"

"No!" His humor was infectious, and against her will Caroline found herself responding to it.

"You do," she insisted, abandoning all formality between then. "I just hope your brother is more tolerant in his attitudes to women."

There was another of those pregnant silences, and Caroline wondered exactly what she had said. When he replied there was little humor left in his voice. "Oh, yes," he said, and she heard the irony in his tone, "Esteban is much more tolerant, you will find. It was he who employed you, *señorita*. How could he think otherwise?"

It was not the answer she would have preferred, and she was left feeling decidedly deflated. For a few minutes she had lost the feeling of apprehension that had gripped her ever since Señor Allende had burst into her room. But once again a sense of unease enveloped her, making her overwhelmingly aware of her own vulnerability.

"How—how much farther is it?" she asked now,

needing his voice to dispel her tension. He frowned into the darkness. "Not far," he told her. "Five miles at most. Are you tired? Or perhaps hungry? I am sure my brother's housekeeper will have a meal waiting for you."

"And—and your aunt?" Caroline probed. "Señora Garcia told me she also lives at the—the hacienda."

"That is correct. She came to San Luis when my father married her sister. She has never married, and she considers San Luis her home."

Caroline welcomed this information. An elderly aunt sounded infinitely less intimidating than a man whose wife had died in childbirth, and who might or might not have mourned her passing. She stared out blindly into the darkness. It seemed such a long way. The road was so bad and so twisting. Was this the only link with civilization?

She was not thinking of what she was doing, slumped in her seat, wrapped in the corkscrewing spiral of her thoughts. Consequently, when the Range Rover swung around a bend in the road and Señor Montejo braked hard to avoid a pile of rocks and debris brought down by the rain, she was flung around like a doll, cracking her head on the windscreen before being thrown back against him. It happened so suddenly that she was unable to save herself, and she clutched at him violently to prevent further punishment.

"¡Dios mio!" he muttered as the vehicle shuddered to a standstill, and his arm automatically went around her. "Are you all right? Did I hurt you? I am sorry. This road can be treacherous after a storm."

Caroline breathed shakily, her face pressed against the soft material of his shirt. Beneath the fine cloth his heart was pounding heavily in her ears, and the clean male scent of his skin filled her nostrils. His body was hard, muscular, unyielding, and yet possessed of a supple strength that accommodated the flexibility of hers. Even after the Range Rover had ground to a halt and the uncanny silence had enveloped them in its blanketing shield, she clung to his strength and knew it was not just the near accident that had aroused such a desire for his protection.

"Miss Leyton!" His voice was a key lower, husky, possessed of a certain restraint. "Miss Leyton, what is it? Are you hurt? Tell me, what is the matter?"

His words brought Caroline to her senses, and with a little gesture of negation she moved away from him. Immediately he withdrew his arm from the back of her seat and, after allowing her a swift appraisal, thrust open his door.

Sliding his arms into his jacket, he retrieved a spade from the back of the vehicle, and while she endeavored to compose herself he vigorously disposed of the pile of debris. He worked in the illumination of the headlights, bending, lifting and throwing the contents of the spade across the ditch at the side of the road. Caroline watched him with uneasy awareness, troubled as much by her own reactions to him as by their brush with danger. It was disturbing to realize that during those moments in his arms she had known a wholly unexpected sense of anticipation, and she knew that if he had chosen to bend his head and find her mouth with his, she would not have objected.

It was a shocking realization, not only because of her feelings for Andrew, but because she had known Luis Montejo for such a short period of time. She had thought herself so self-confident, so emancipated—yet when the warm scent of his breath had brushed her cheek she had felt as weak and susceptible as any Victorian miss. She checked the shoulder-length curve of her hair with unsteady fingers. No doubt he had known how she felt, she thought with some self-derision. He must be highly amused now, after her previous assertions of female rights. Perhaps she should be grateful he had not chosen to take advantage of the situation. It would have been doubly humiliating to arrive on Don Esteban's doorstep with his brother's brand already upon her.

The spade thudded into the back of the vehicle and she stiffened as the door beside her opened and Montejo climbed back into his seat. This time he kept his jacket on, the damp smell of the material mingling with the faint odor of sweat from his exertions.

"You are sure you are all right?" he inquired again, his voice perceptibly cooler now, yet still polite and concerned.

She nodded, fingering a slight swelling on her temple. "I should have been more careful," she murmured, endeavoring to keep her tone light. "Your roads are certainly—unpredictable."

"And dangerous," he agreed with grim impatience, starting the engine abruptly and thrusting the shift into drive. She turned her head away from him to gaze through the rain-smeared window.

San Luis de Merced was a village as well as the place where Don Estaban de Montejo had his estates. There were lights in the village, glowing through the shutters of adobe dwellings, mingling with the smoke from a dozen chimneys. There was the spicy smell of meat and peppers, and the stronger aroma of wood smoke. Children stopped in open doorways to watch their progress. Someone shouted after them, and Montejo answered, raising his hand in greeting as Caroline thought she heard the word *padre*. But her attention was diverted as the Range Rover lurched onto an upward slope, and she clung desperately to her seat as they wound precipitously up through a belt of trees to where high wooden gates were set in a gray stone wall. The wall itself was easily eight feet high, a solid barrier to what was beyond, and Caroline's nerves tightened. Beyond the wall was her destination, and her courage faltered at the sight of that prisonlike edifice.

Montejo brought the vehicle to a halt and sprang down again to hammer on the gates. Reassuringly, they were soon opened by an elderly retainer dressed in the usual garb of loose-fitting pants and waistcoat, the sleeves of his shirt rolled back to his elbows. He removed the wide-brimmed hat from his head as they drove through, and then replaced it again to close the gates behind them.

"Gomez," remarked her companion shortly as Caroline glanced back over her shoulder. "He used to work for my brother, but now he is too old to ride herd and spends his days keeping the gate."

"Like Saint Peter," murmured Caroline, wishing to ease the tension inside her.

Montejo gave her a thoughtful look. "Perhaps," he conceded at length, but Caroline had the distinct impression he had been tempted to make another comparison.

Beyond the gates the tires encountered the solid mass of a stone courtyard. Caroline decided it resembled an ancient fortress with its outer walls and solid buttresses, a width of drive leading past stables and outbuildings and under an inner archway to the stone-flagged entrance.

Montejo drove under the arch and brought the Range Rover to a halt at the foot of a flight of steps leading up to a wooden door. The rain had ceased and the warmth of the night air dispelled the feeling of chill Caroline had developed when first she saw the house. There was the fragrant scent of oleander and hibiscus, and the soft smell of earth after rain. As she climbed out of the vehicle Caroline determined not to allow what had happened in Las Estadas to influence her first impressions of her home for the next few weeks.

The door above them opened as Montejo was unloading her cases from the Range-Rover. A plump, round-faced little woman descended the steps to greet them, and meeting her round, beady little eyes, Caroline wondered if this could be Doña Isabel. She was quickly disillusioned.

"Consuella," remarked the man beside her, straightening with a case in each hand. "She speaks little English, but she will do her best."

"*Buenos tardes, señor.*" Consuella addressed herself

to Montejo, but her eyes were all for Caroline. "*Buenos tardes, señorita. Bienvenido a San Luis.*"

"Thank you—*gracias*!" It was one of the few words she knew, and Caroline glanced in some embarrassment toward Señor Montejo, doubting the accuracy of her accent.

But he merely inclined his head and said, "*Muy bien*," in a low voice behind her, as they followed the gesticulating Consuella up the steps. "*No sabia que podia hablar espanol*!" he added, confusing her further.

She glanced around at him, pursing her lips. "You must know I don't understand you," she whispered, aware of Consuella's inquisitive interest, and his smile was a disturbing reminder of the way he had made her feel in the car.

"*No importa*," he assured her, his meaning obvious this time, and she sighed. "Esteban was educated at Oxford. I am sure you will have no difficulty in understanding him."

The undertones of his words were lost on her as she stepped into the baroque beauty of the exquisitely decorated hall of the house. In the light of a dozen electric lamps concealed behind bronze shades her eyes were dazzled by fluted columns supporting the high-arched ceiling, by heavily carved moldings and inlaid mosaics and by miniaturized statues of the Virgin and Child. The vertiginous twists of a wrought-iron staircase were enhanced by leaves veined in marble, and the checkerboard pattern beneath their feet was colored in black and gold. If the outer appearance of the house had been daunting, its inner beauty more than made up for it. She turned to the man behind her with bewildered eyes, seeking some explanation;

"As you can see, my brother lives in style, *señorita*," Montejo remarked mockingly, and before she could make any protest at his own apparent acceptance of the situation, another voice broke in on them.

"Señorita Leyton?" it inquired in vaguely slurred

tones. "It is Señorita Leyton, is it not? ¡Hola! Welcome to the Hacienda Montejo, *señorita*. I hope you are going to be very happy here."

Caroline turned half-guiltily, aware of the disloyalty of her thoughts only moments before, to find a man approaching them across the expanse of black-and-gold marble. If this was Esteban Montejo, and she had every reason to suppose it was, he, too, was tall, though not as tall as his brother and of much heavier build. He was immaculately dressed in a formal evening suit of seamed black pants and white jacket, matching his surroundings, his only apparent concession to the heat being the printed silk cravat around his throat instead of the usual white tie. But what disturbed Caroline most was the unevenness of his approach; the way he placed each foot with evident precision, and the faintly smug expression he adopted as he neared her.

"My brother, Don Esteban," observed Luis Montejo with studied politeness, and Caroline felt her hand captured and raised almost to Don Esteban's lips.

"I am most happy to meet you, *señorita*," Don Esteban assured her ardently, and the odor on his breath was unmistakable. Was this the indisposition his brother had hinted at, Caroline wondered faintly, smothering her revulsion. She knew a moment's incredulity that the features that had so much in common should be so amazingly different.

Realizing she had to say something to retrieve her hand, she forced a smile. "You—you have a beautiful home, *señor*," she murmured, determinedly withdrawing her fingers from his. "It—well, it's not at all what I expected."

Don Esteban rocked back on his heels, casting a satisfied glance toward the intricately carved ceiling, the white walls and pilasters, the iron balustrade that formed a gallery above them. "You like it?" he drawled with consummate ease. "It is a modest dwelling compared to the palaces my family left behind them in Cadiz, *señorita*." He shrugged. "But—" and here his dark eyes, much darker than those of his brother, returned to her face "—it serves the purpose. And there is room enough for the three members of my family who live here."

"Oh, but—" Caroline's brows ascended and she glanced in some confusion toward the man who had brought her here. How could there be only three members?

And as if understanding that silent inquiry, Don Esteban spoke again. "My brother?" he suggested. "Luis?" His tongue slurred over the man's name. "Did he not tell you, *señorita*? Did he not explain?" His lips curled. "My brother does not live with us here at San Luis, Miss Leyton. Like his namesake, Luis is in search of immortality. He lives in Mariposa, *señorita*. At the seminary of San Pedro de Alcantara."

CHAPTER TWO

CAROLINE AWAKENED with the instinctive awareness that all was not well. For a few minutes she lay still in the middle of the huge baroque bed with its carved headboard and gilded hangings—once used, Don Esteban had assured her, by the emperor Maximilian himself—and let the events of the previous evening sweep over her in intimate detail. And then, loath to spoil the new day with such reminiscences, she thrust back the silken coverings and put her feet to the floor.

There was a rug beside her bed, a soft, silky alpaca rug into which her toes curled, and she allowed its sensuous touch to soothe her unquiet thoughts. No matter what she had let herself into here, she was committed to stay for at least four weeks, she told herself severely. But it was not an easy fact to accept.

The night before had been like something out of a dream, or perhaps "nightmare" described it more aptly. Remembering the dinner she had shared with the two brothers, she shuddered in revulsion, and her palms found her cheeks as she recalled that grotesque meal in its entirety.

It had been obvious from the start that Don Esteban was by no means sober, and the amount of wine served with the meal had only exaggerated his condition. They had eaten in the ornate dining room, at a table large enough to seat a score of guests, and from silver and crystal worth a small fortune. They were served by an army of waiters, and offered a fantastic number of courses, each cooked and presented with a different sauce. There were several courses of fish, from a spicy stuffed variety to the lightest of shellfish mousses, chilled soups, steaming consommés, wine-flavored and aromatic, chicken served in wine and cream, stuffed tamales, enchiladas deliciously filled with cheese, pork and served with apples and tomatoes and onions, and every kind of fruit imaginable.

Caroline had eaten little, aware of the dangers of too much rich food on a stomach already churning with nerves, and she had noticed that Don Esteban followed her example. But he had continually filled his glass, watching her intently across the expanse of polished mahogany, probing and assessing, making her overwhelmingly aware that he found her presence at his table pleasing to him.

Luis Montejo had eaten more enthusiastically, drinking only a little wine, keeping his thoughts to himself. It had been left to Caroline to answer Don Esteban's questions, and to listen in shocked fascination as he deliberately proceeded to provoke his brother.

Remembering it all now, Caroline rose from the bed and padded barefoot across to the window. Without the benefit of the rug, the tiled floor was cool to her feet, but she scarcely noticed. Drawing the heavy curtains aside, she opened the window and gasped with sudden wonder at the beauty of the view.

Last night there had been nothing to be seen, only darkness and the troubling obscurity of her own thoughts. But this morning the sun was shining, and even the enclosing wall that surrounded the property had taken on a rose-colored hue.

But it was beyond the wall that Caroline's eyes were drawn, to the flower-strewn banks of a river flowing through rugged but open land to where a church tower stood silhouetted against the sky. Her eyes followed the river as it rushed through a narrow gorge to disappear from sight, only to appear again in the shimmering distance, a spreading, shifting expanse of water. Caroline blinked. That was no river, she realized in sudden excitement. It was the sea. Only the sea could give that blue green tinge to the horizon, and her spirits soared.

She had known Yucatan was a peninsula, but somehow she had never imagined San Luis de Merced might be near the sea. She gazed at it eagerly, savoring its familiarity, and breathed deeply as if she could already taste its salty flavor.

With an effort she allowed her attention to be caught by a movement near at hand. There was a herd of cattle grazing some distance from the house, and her eyes widened at their number. There must be hundreds, she thought incredulously, and then wondered with some misgivings if one had to negotiate the herds to reach the estuary.

She sighed. No doubt she would find out. But once again the more immediate present gripped her, reminding her that she had yet to meet her charge, the young Emilia, or the elderly retainer, Doña Isabel.

There was a bathroom adjoining the bedroom, and checking that it was still quite early, barely eight o'clock in fact, she went to take a shower. She had been too exhausted the night before to do anything more than wash her face and hands and clean her teeth, but now she surveyed the bathroom's luxurious appointments with more enthusiasm.

Like everything else, the bathroom was ornate. The walls were lined with gilded mirrors, the taps on the bath and washbasin were gold plated, and even the shower had a gold-plated spray. Still the water was hot, and refusing to allow the memory of how the majority of the population lived to deter her, Caroline pulled on a shower cap and stepped beneath the invigorating cascade.

Toweling herself dry, she returned to the bedroom again, viewing her still packed cases with some distaste. They would have to wait until she discovered what her duties were going to be, she decided, and determinedly dismissed the fleeting urge to beg Luis to take her with him when he left for Mariposa.

Dropping the towel, she rummaged for clean underwear, but when she turned back, the shred of cream cot-

ton clutched in her hand, she encountered her reflection
in the long gilded cheval mirrors. They were very nar-
cissistic mirrors, she realized, folding one upon the
other, throwing back her image from every angle. But
they were candid, too, in their search for perfection,
and there was no way one could disguise any possible
flaw.

Reluctantly Caroline allowed herself a moment's
assessment, half turning to profile the upward thrust of
her breasts. They were not pendulous breasts, but firm
and rounded, the nipples hard after the vigorous toweling she had given herself. Her body was slim without
being angular, her hips shapely, her legs long and attractive. She sometimes thought her legs were her best
feature, although Andrew had insisted she had equally
desirable attributes elsewhere. Her tongue circled lips
that were unknowingly sensuous, troubled a little by her
thoughts at that moment. It was not of Andrew that she
was thinking, but of Luis de Montejo, and her own
disturbing awareness of him as a man. She had never
met a man quite like him before, but then she had never
had a conversation with a Roman Catholic priest
before. The Reverend Mr. Thomas, the Church of
England vicar at St. David's back home, bore no resemblance to the man who had rescued her from Señor
Allende's unwanted attentions, and even now she found
it difficult to associate Luis with the church.

Luis! The way his name came so easily to her tongue
was disturbing, too, and she drew her lower lip between
her teeth, nibbling on it uneasily. Unwillingly she recalled Don Esteban's behavior over dinner. His attitude
toward his brother had been deliberately offensive and,
as the evening progressed, increasingly crude. He had
spoken of things in Caroline's presence that even she, in
her self-asserted role of emancipist, would have preferred not to hear, and she had badly wanted to escape.
When he baited Luis, when he made a mockery of his
tolerance of the people, when he spoke of his celibacy,
Caroline had wanted to die of embarrassment; but Don

Esteban had seemed to enjoy her discomfort far more than his brother's indifference.

And Luis had maintained a facade of detachment, whether it was real or otherwise. He had refused to answer his brother's coarser comments and had adopted an air of resigned fortitude that succeeded inasmuch as it seemed to drive Don Esteban almost to distraction. Don Esteban's speech became fouler, he filled his glass more frequently, and finally he slumped in his chair, the victim of his own frustration. Several of the servants came at once to carry him to bed, almost as if this was a regular occurrence, and Caroline was left to face Luis's intent appraisal, with the distinct perception of her own inadequacy.

She had wanted to rant at him then, to accuse him of knowing to what he was bringing her, to question his integrity in allowing her to believe that his brother was an ordinary man—but she hadn't. How could she blame him for her own foolhardiness? How could she despise him when she had chosen this job? If anyone was to blame it was Señora Garcia, for deceiving her so completely; although even that imposition didn't hold water when Caroline considered how ambiguously the advertisement had been worded. It was her own fault and hers alone. She had accepted the post, and come here with a high opinion of her own capabilities, and if it proved to be a disaster, then she would have to extricate herself.

She gave a grim little smile now as she recalled their conversation on the way to San Luis de Merced. What must he have been thinking when she made her stand for women's liberation? How subtly he had avoided discussing his brother's position. He must have known how soon her eyes would be opened, and yet not then, or last evening, or had he voiced the obvious cliché.

With an exclamation of impatience, she put on her scanty underwear and reached for the simple pleat- ed skirt folded on top of her suitcase. The matching silk shirt was the color of African violets, and the outfit was in sharp contrast to the pale fall of ash-blond hair. Her

hair was straight and silky, smooth from a center parting, and ideal in this climate where more elaborate styles
would droop with the humidity. She could wash it and
let it dry naturally in an hour.

She was smoothing a shiny lip gloss onto her mouth
when there was a knock at her door. Half turning, she
called, "Come in!"

After a few moments' pause, the door was tentatively
opened. A young Indian girl stood just outside, holding
a tray. Attired in the black dress and white apron that
seemed to be uniform for all the female staff, she
ducked her head politely and said, "*El desayuno, por
favor, señorita. ¿Puedo entrar?*"

Caroline put down her lip brush and smiled. "You
can put the tray over there," she said, indicating the
marble-topped table near the windows, and then, summoning what little of the language she could remember,
she added, "*¿Tu nombre—qué es?*"

The girl put down the tray and straightened nervously, folding her hands together. "*Carmencita, señorita,*"
she answered, the wide dark eyes darting around the
room. "*¿Puedo salir ahora?*"

Caroline sighed. She wasn't absolutely sure, but she
guessed Carmencita had orders not to gossip with the
new governess, and spreading her hands, she gave the
girl permission to leave.

With the door closed again, she approached the tray
with some misgivings. She would have preferred to go
downstairs, to accustom herself to her new surroundings before she was summoned to meet her charge, but
obviously she was obliged to follow orders. So she lifted
the silver cloches that protected hot rolls and scrambled
eggs, tasted the peach preserve, and poured some rich
black coffee into a cup of china so fine that it was
almost transparent.

Then, summoning all her composure, she opened her
door and let herself into the corridor outside. The night
before, Consuella had escorted her to her room, bidden
by Luis de Montejo after his brother's undignified

departure. Whatever his position in the house, Luis's word appeared to carry as much weight as that of Don Esteban, and Caroline suspected that the staff respected him more. Two brothers could hardly have been more different, yet the result was the same. And did it really matter to these people?

The long hall stretched ahead of her, its stonework inlaid with panels of carving and interspersed with portraits of long-dead Montejos. Overhead the ceiling was an arch of heavily embossed molding, and because it was without windows it was constantly lighted by a series of gothic sconces, each accommodating an electric bulb. It was curious, but the night before she had scarcely been aware of the eerie isolation of this part of the house, those painted eyes in their canvas sockets troubling her not at all. But this morning the remoteness of her rooms from the rest of the hacienda seemed infinitely significant, and she could not dispel the realization that she was completely without support here.

She hurried along the corridor, her heels silent on the softly piled carpet that unrolled its length in shades of black and gold, and emerged at the head of the staircase with a feeling of having navigated a particularly treacherous expanse of ocean.

Thinking of the nearness of the ocean, she endeavored to dismiss her foolish fears. She was allowing the house and its lavish appointments to influence her impressions of her employer, and the sooner she found a true perspective the better.

Downstairs she encountered some of the servants already at work, polishing the massive width of the hall on bended knees. They looked up curiously as she hesitated, uncertain of her destination, and then the sound of a child's laughter erased the last traces of irresolution. Nothing was more delightful than the spontaneous laughter of a child, she thought, crossing the hall in the direction of the voices she could now hear. Don Esteban must hold some affection in his daughter's eyes at least, and she was relieved to have the burden of indecision lifted from her.

But when she reached the arched doorway that led into a huge sunlit salon, she faltered once again. Sure enough her charge was there—a small, plump little girl, extravagantly arrayed in a white dress with layer upon layer of frills, overset by strings of pink ribbon—but the man who was on all fours, and on whose back she was energetically riding, was not her father.

"Ah, Miss Leyton! Good morning!"

With a lithe effort Luis de Montejo swung the child down from his back and got easily to his feet, quelling the little girl's protests with a soothing hand on her long black hair. In the same moleskin pants he had worn the night before, but this time with a cream silk shirt to complement them, he was relaxed and magnetic, a vibrant masculine being with the unmistakable glow of good health. His shirt had become partially unbuttoned during his antics on the floor and now his long fingers probed to fasten it, but not before Caroline had observed the dark arrowing of fine body hair that disappeared below his belt.

"Tío Vincente, Tío Vincente!" Emilia, for this was evidently Don Esteban's daughter, tugged impotently at his sleeve. "¿Quien es?" she exclaimed, subjecting Caroline to a malevolent scrutiny from beneath dark brows. "¿Qué desea? ¡Ella no me gusta!"

"Hush, little one. Speak in English, remember?" Luis exhorted her softly, restraining her sulky tirade. "Miss Leyton is here to teach you your numbers, as you know very well. And I do not wish to hear that you have been rude to her."

Emilia's lips pursed. "I know my numbers," she declared in perfect English, surprising Caroline by her lack of accent. "Miss Thackeray taught me my numbers, and my letters, and I do not need any more teachers."

Miss Thackeray? Caroline's brow furrowed. Had Miss Thackeray been her predecessor, and if so, why was she no longer here?

"Miss Thackeray used to be my governess," Luis inserted dryly, correctly interpreting Caroline's little frown. "She lived at San Luis from the time I was six years old, but unfortunately she died last year, and since then Emilia has had no formal education."

"I see." Caroline endeavored to hide her relief. For an awful moment she had wondered if she was the last in a succession of governesses, all of whom had objected to living at the hacienda.

"You won't like it here at San Luis," Emilia stated now, abandoning her pleas to her uncle and turning instead to the offensive. "There are snakes, and spiders, and bats that suck your blood!" She twisted her face into a horrifying grimace. "Do you believe in vampires, Miss Leyton? Because if you do not, you must be as stupid as you look!" And brushing past Caroline, she ran out of the room before either her governess or her uncle could prevent her.

"Well!" Left alone once again with Luis, Caroline felt hopelessly embarrassed, as much by her own sense of inadequacy as by what the child had said. "What do I do now?"

Luis's mouth compressed. "You are asking me?"

"Who else?" Caroline made an encompassing gesture around the otherwise empty room. "There is no one else." She expelled her breath unevenly. "Is she always like that?"

Luis shrugged, tucking his thumbs into the back of his belt. "You must make allowances for Emilia. She has had a rather—unusual upbringing."

"That I can believe!" Caroline was vehement.

"Do not misunderstand me, Miss Leyton. I am not saying that Emilia is without gentleness, compassion. Only that she has never known a mother's care."

Caroline shook her head. "But your aunt—"

"Tiá Isabel is—how shall I say it—a little unworldly." he paused. "Miss Thackeray was the fulcrum of Emilia's existence. When she died...."

"But what about her father?" Caroline had to say it.

"Surely he—" She broke off and then said inconsequently, "For brothers, you are totally different."

"Forgive me—" Luis's gray eyes narrowed "—but is that one of your famous English non sequiturs? I do not see what relevance it has to the purpose."

"It hasn't," Caroline murmured forlornly, bending her head. "I mean, it has no relevance, of course. I just wish—" She broke off again. "Are there really vampire bats here?"

Luis's mouth softened a little. "And if I say yes, will you go running back to Mérida?"

He was teasing her, but she could not respond to it. "Perhaps, if I could," she answered now, and his sudden humor disappeared behind a mask of gravity.

"I think I must be going," he said, moving purposefully toward the door. "I promised Tomas I would ride with him this morning, and it grows late."

"Wait—" Caroline went after him urgently, her green eyes wide and anxious. "Please, you have to tell me—what am I to do about Emilia? Where is she? When do her lessons begin? And. . .and are we allowed to go outside the grounds of the hacienda?"

Luis halted in the doorway and looked down at her with studied consideration. His stillness disturbed her. The penetration of those light eyes was disruptive. Her lungs began to feel constricted and her throat felt tight, and she wondered if this was how a penitent felt in the presence of a confessor.

"I suggest you ask my brother these things," he advised her at last, his voice curiously constrained. "He is your employer, *señorita*, not I. Now, if you will permit me—"

"You're not. . .leaving?"

It seemed imperative that she should know this for a fact, and without really thinking what she was doing she followed Emilia's example and gripped his sleeve. Only somehow her fingers encountered the hair-roughened skin of his forearm, and the feeling of the taut muscle beneath his skin caused an involuntary tremor of awareness to ripple through her. She looked down at her fingers, spreading them almost experimentally, and then her chin jerked upward as he wrenched his arm out of her grasp.

"I return to Mariposa in three days, *señorita*," he told her harshly, and without another word he strode away.

Caroline turned back into the salon, aware that she was trembling. She realized she had done an unforgivable thing by making him aware of her like that, but it had happened completely without her volition. Yet perhaps it was inevitable. He was the only person she could turn to, and she dreaded the thought of his eventual departure. But somehow she had to face that reality, and live with it.

"*Señorita!*"

For a moment the whispered use of her name confused her. She had thought herself alone in the room. But now she saw that the door to an inner salon had opened and a tiny figure, voluminous in folds of black silk, was hovering on the threshold. A headdress, of the kind Caroline had previously only seen on those ancient portraits upstairs, formed a kind of jeweled halo above the woman's coiled hair, and her ears and the gnarled knuckles of her fingers glittered with a veritable fortune in diamonds, rubies and emeralds.

"Doña Isabel?" ventured Caroline nervously, at a loss to know how else to address her, and the tiny figure bobbed her head in assent. "How—how do you do? I'm Caroline Leyton. Er—Emilia's new governess."

"Governess, pah!" Doña Isabel released her hold on the door and advanced a few paces into the room, staring at Caroline with unconcealed contempt. "I know who you are, señorita" she admonished her in a low guttural undertone. "You are Esteban's latest *puta*, that is who you are! Do you think you can deceive me? No, I have lived here too long!"

Caroline was astounded. Her knowledge of Spanish might not be comprehensive, but she knew exactly what *puta* meant, and its connotations were not only shocking but insulting.

"I assure you, Doña Isabel—" she began, only to have the old lady interrupt her.

"Be silent! I do not hold conversations with *putas*!" she hissed arrogantly. "How dare you enter my sister's sitting room? How dare you show your legs, like any common—"

"That will do, Tía Isabel." The cultivated masculine tones came as such a relief that Caroline turned to face her employer with real gratitude in her face. She was fast coming to the conclusion that no one could remain sane in this madhouse, and to see Don Esteban entering the room, apparently composed and sober, in his elegant gray business suit, seemed almost a miracle.

"¡Puta! ¡Puta!" cried Doña Isabel shrilly, her voice rising in her agitation. "How dare Esteban permit his women to use my sister's—"

"Tía Isabel, my father is dead," declared Don Esteban flatly, spreading his hands apologetically in Caroline's direction. "*Señorita*, please forgive my aunt. She is sometimes—forgetful."

Caroline shook her head in bewilderment as the old lady frowned and tried to absorb what her nephew was saying. "Esteban is dead?" she echoed, thin brows meeting above a long aquiline nose. "Then—then who is this girl? What is she doing at San Luis de Merced?"

"Miss Leyton is Emilia's new governess," explained her nephew calmly. "You remember? I told you. She has come from England to teach Emilia the geography and the history, no?"

Doña Isabel viewed Caroline with some suspicion. "But she was here, talking with Luis. I saw the way she looked at him!"

"You are imagining things, *mi tía*," Esteban retorted, evidently losing patience. "Go back to your embroidery, *tía*; I wish to discuss business matters with Miss Leyton."

Doña Isabel hesitated, but clearly Esteban had the

upper hand, and with a gesture that was curiously pathetic, she disappeared out the door through which she had entered. Her departure was a definite relief, and Caroline linked her fingers together in an effort to hide their obvious trembling, wishing she had more experience in these matters.

"Please sit down." Esteban was all sympathetic affability now. "I do not know how I can satisfactorily atone for my aunt's behavior, except to beg your indulgence for her temporary lapses of memory." He sighed. "She is—was—my mother's sister; an unmarried lady of uncertain years, and prone, I regret to say, to periods of fantasy concerning my father's behavior."

Caroline, who had subsided gratefully onto a satin-striped sofa, looked up at him. "You mean—your father is the Esteban she talks about?"

"That is correct. I was named for him."

"I see." Caroline nodded.

"And, of course, Isabel was a little jealous of her sister's good fortune." He smiled, showing even white teeth, brilliant in his dark face. "Is it not always the way with unmarried ladies?"

Caroline made an awkward gesture, not quite knowing how to answer him, and taking advantage of her momentary confusion, he sat down on the sofa beside her, his bulk causing the cushions to slope a little in his direction.

"¡Señorita!" He looked diffident, and for a moment she thought he was going to apologize for his own behavior the night before, but he didn't. "Señorita, I am so glad you have come here. Emilia—my daughter, you understand—is sorely in need of young companionship. I do not know how much Doña Elena—Señora Garcia, that is—told you, but since my wife's death Emilia has been brought up by an elderly countrywoman of yours, a Miss Thackeray."

"Yes." Caroline acknowledged this without explaining how she was so informed.

He went on eagerly, "She was not a good influence

on the child, *señorita*. Many times she went against my judgment in matters concerning Emilia, and unfortunately, my brother, Luis, took her part."

"I see." This was deeper water. "I'm sorry."

"So am I." Esteban was grave. "Luis and I are brothers, and it is always sad when blood turns against blood."

"Oh, I'm sure—" began Caroline awkwardly, only to break off abruptly when Esteban raised his hand.

"You do not yet understand, Miss Leyton. Just as Tía Isabel was jealous of her sister, so Luis is jealous of me."

"No—"

"But yes. I regret that it is so." And indeed, Esteban did look melancholy. "I am the elder brother, *entiende*? I have inherited our father's estate. Luis has nothing, except what I give him. His mother, you see, was the *puta* of whom Tía Isabel speaks."

Caroline's face felt frozen in an attitude of disbelief, and as if realizing he had gone too far, Esteban hastened to retract.

"Forgive me," he said as she shrank back against the cushions. "I should not have told you so brutally. I do not mean to be—callous, but I cannot forget that it was Luis's mother who caused my mother's death. She killed herself, you know, *mi madre*. She flung herself from a second-floor window down to the courtyard beneath." He massaged his temples with the middle finger and the thumb of one hand. "Believe me, that is not something one can easily forget."

"But—" Caroline swallowed convulsively. "Your—your brother's name is Montejo."

"Oh, yes." Esteban heaved a heavy sigh. "My father married Luis's mother—afterward. My brother is no bastard, *señorita*. At least—" he paused "—he is not illegitimate."

CHAPTER THREE

CAROLINE AND HER CHARGE were to work in the library.

After unburdening himself of the reasons for the antipathy between himself and Luis, Esteban became calm and businesslike. With a sense of pride, in complete contrast to his inconsequence of the night before, he showed Caroline around the main rooms of the hacienda, pointing out particular pieces of interest and relating a little of their history. He was knowledgeable about the myths and legends of the area, making her blood tingle with stories of mindless clay men created by the gods, of soulless wooden men whose tools rose up in rebellion against them and who were turned into monkeys. He showed her an Aztec funerary mask and described how the evil goddess Tezcatlipoca had dressed the god Quetzalcoatl in such a mask before forcing him to take part in a drunken orgy of lust and incest. The culmination had been that Quetzalcoatl had flung himself onto a funeral pyre, and after several days of purification his heart had risen to the heavens to become the planet Venus.

There were many such legends, each attached to some remnant of history. While some artifacts bore the overwhelming influence of Catholicism, others reflected the country's original pagan traditions. There were tiny effigies of Totec, the Mayan god of mankind; Yum Caax, the maize god; Kinich Ahau and Tlacolteutl; Xolotl, Quetzalcoatl's brother; and Hanhau, the Mayan god of death. The hacienda was a treasure house of gold and antiquity, and although there was something slightly vulgar about it, it was undeniably impressive.

It was while they were examining the *azulejos*, the

glazed blue tiles in the music room, that Caroline
became aware of someone watching them, and turning
quickly, she saw Emilia hovering reluctantly in the
doorway. Esteban turned and saw her, too, and with a
gesture of welcome he bid her join them.

"Come, *pequeña*," he beckoned her affably. "Come
and meet Miss Leyton. She is your new governess, and I
want you to be friends."

Emilia made no move toward them. Clearly Esteban
had not been lying when he'd said she disobeyed him,
but whether that was through Luis's influence or not,
there was no way of knowing—yet. Certainly Luis's affection for the little girl had seemed genuine enough,
and hers for him, but until Caroline had had a chance to
talk with the child she could make no real assessment.

"Emilia! *¡Venga! ¡Immediatamente!*" Esteban's
voice had lost a lot of its benevolence. "Come—see
what I have here for you." He fumbled in his pocket as
if searching for a gift. "If you do not come and look,
you will never know what it is I have here, will you?
Now—are you going to do as you are told?"

Emilia sighed and then, evidently curious to know
what he was holding, she left her position by the door
and approached them with measured steps. She scarcely
looked at Caroline. Her attention was all concentrated
on her father, and as she neared him she tilted her head
slightly, trying to see what he had in his hand.

Caroline was curious, too, but she stepped aside
politely, unwilling to intrude on this exchange between
father and daughter. It was the first time she had seen
them together; although there was a faint family
resemblance, Emilia's features must more closely resem-
ble those of her mother, she decided.

What happened next happened so suddenly that it
was over before she could protest, even had she dared to
do so. As Emilia stretched out her neck to glimpse
what her father was holding, his hand shot out and
caught her, biting into her arm with cruel intent as his
other hand delivered a blow to her cheek. Emilia stag-

gered and would have fallen had he not been holding her. Her face went white, as white as the muslin of her dress, except for the livid marks of her father's fingers that were rapidly reddening, but she did not cry. Caroline could see her steeling herself, forcing back the tears, and realized, as the blood drained from her own face, that she was holding her breath.

She expelled it as Don Esteban caught his daughter's chin between his fingers, forcing her face up to his. "Let that be a lesson to you, *pequeña*," he declared with cold emphasis. "You will not make a fool of me in front of Miss Leyton, as you tried to do with Miss Thackeray!"

"No, *señor*."

Emilia spoke respectfully, but her voice was sullen. It was obvious from her behavior, that this was not the first time her father had struck her, but she had learned from experience not to answer back.

"Now—greet Miss Leyton as the daughter of the house of Montejo should do, with politeness and courtesy and a smile on that sulky little face of yours," he advised, and Caroline had to face yet another mortifying moment.

"Welcome to San Luis de Merced, Miss Leyton," Emilia recited, her eyes downcast. And then, at her father's insistence, she lifted her head and spread her lips in an unholy rictus. "I hope you will be very happy here."

Caroline gathered herself with difficulty. "Thank you, Emilia," she replied stiffly. "I—hope I will be, too."

"So now that the formalities are over, we will show Miss Leyton where you are to work," announced Don Esteban, releasing his daughter's arm. "I think you will find my choice of venue appealing, Miss Leyton. The library is a soundproof room, and I have many interesting first editions."

The library was as impressive as the rest of the house. Books lined the walls from floor to ceiling, leather bound and highly polished, their gold lettering as distinctive now as it had ever been.

"As you can see, I insist that this collection be kept in

perfect condition,'' Esteban said proudly. "From time to time I have an expert come here from the university in Mexico City. He examines the books and arranges any restorative work that is necessary.''

Caroline looked around her in admiration. A tiny iron-railed balcony was situated near the molded ceiling, allowing any enthusiastic bibliophile access to the upper shelves, and a delicately carved spiral staircase complemented the mobile ladder that provided a means of reaching the more remote volumes.

"You will work here.'' Esteban indicated a leather-topped desk set beneath the long windows. "See—I have arranged for Emilia's books to be placed here for your perusal, and if you require anything further, it can be obtained from the supplier in Mérida.''

"Thank you.'' Caroline touched the pile of worn textbooks with a grateful finger. This, at least, was something she knew and understood, and she glanced anxiously at Emilia, expecting to meet resentment or antagonism. But Emilia returned her gaze with only faintly hostile eyes, and Caroline's spirits lifted slightly at the prospect of making some headway.

"I will leave you,'' Esteban said now, much to her relief. "I have matters of the estate to discuss with my overseer. I will see you both at lunchtime, *señorita*, when we can discuss Emilia's progress. Until then, *hasta luego*, Miss Leyton. *Hasta luego*, Emilia.''

The door closed and Caroline sank down rather weakly onto the leather chair beside the desk. The silence that followed Esteban's departure was pregnant with emotion, but anything was better than the tension that had gripped her since Emilia had joined them in the music room.

Emilia moved around the desk now to lean with her elbows on its surface. She regarded Caroline's troubled face with concentration for a few moments and then, with an inconsequence mature for her years, said, "I told you you wouldn't like it here.''

Caroline looked at her blankly and then briskly

reached for one of the dog-eared textbooks. "You know, you could be right," she remarked calmly, and opened the book.

"You didn't tell him," Emilia went on insistently. "You didn't tell Don Esteban what I said. Why not?"

"What you said?" Caroline frowned as if she couldn't remember the child's words in intimate detail. "What did you say?"

Emilia sighed. "You know! About your not liking it here. About the spiders and the vampires!"

"Oh, I see." Caroline shrugged her slim shoulders. "I'd forgotten. Besides, of what interest would that be to your father?"

"Don't call him that!" exclaimed Emilia fiercely. "He's not my father! I hate him!"

"Emilia!" Caroline had to protest now. "He is your father, and you shouldn't say such things about him. It... well, it's rude and ignorant."

Emilia straightened. "Tío Vincente is my father," she declared, causing Caroline's lips to part in stunned disbelief. Was there no end to the revelations she was to be subjected to? "Tío Vincente loved my mother. That's why Don Esteban hates me."

"Oh, don't be so silly, Emilia." Caroline had had enough for one day. "Look, I'm not here to discuss who might or might not have loved your mother. I'm sure your father cared for her very deeply, and just because you're disobedient, and your father punishes you, is no reason for you to go spreading malicious tales that have no basis in fact. You are your father's daughter. It's obvious! Now sit down and stop behaving like a melodramatic two-year-old."

Emilia pursed her lips. "You don't know anything."

"Nor do I want to," retorted Caroline shortly, uncomfortably aware that her motives for feeling that way were not entirely disinterested. She couldn't help remembering Luis's reticence when she had asked about Emilia's mother's death, and his reluctance to discuss his brother's reaction. But, as she had continually to keep telling herself, the personal affairs of the Montejos were nothing to do with her. She determinedly began to ask Emilia questions in an attempt to assess the child's capabilities.

In fact the morning passed quite quickly. Once she became interested in proving what a bright and intelligent pupil she was, Emilia lost that air of antagonistic aggression and showed an entirely more sympathetic side to her nature. She was sharp and intelligent, and although, according to Luis, Miss Thackery had died last year, the child's education was nevertheless far in advance of that of most children of her age. She read well and with expression, and her mental arithmetic was good. If she had a failing, it was that she was sometimes too quick with her answers and in consequence made careless mistakes that given a little more time she would have avoided. She had obviously enjoyed her lessons with Miss Thackeray, and whatever the old lady's failings, as far as Emilia's education was concerned she had done a good job.

Emilia told Caroline that lunch was usually served at one o'clock, so at half-past twelve she dismissed her pupil. She had decided to return to her room and do some of her unpacking as well as attend to her appearance. But when she opened the door to her apartments she found that someone had forestalled her: her clothes had all been hung away and her cases stowed in the closet. Unused to such assiduous attention, Caroline felt somewhat disconcerted, but a swift examination of the drawers and wardrobe assured her that her belongings had been handled with the utmost care and consideration.

Examining her reflection in the dressing-table mirror, she noted the faint flush that still lingered in her cheeks—a reminder of the disturbing morning she had spent. She brushed a pale powder compound across the revealing color in an attempt to disguise her agitation and then reapplied the lip gloss to her mouth. In truth, she did feel a little hungry now, having refused a cup of chocolate midmorning, but the prospect of seeing Luis again, after his brother's revelations, tightened the muscles of her throat.

She traversed the length of the corridor again and descended the stairs at ten minutes to one, only to encounter the subject of her nervous speculations in the hall. Luis had evidently just come in from riding, for he was wearing black leather gaucho pants and an open-necked black shirt, and the scent of horseflesh was unmistakable as he moved to pass her and climb the stairs.

"I trust you have had an enjoyable morning, *señorita*," he remarked with his innate courtesy.

Caroline had a hysterical desire to laugh in his face. An enjoyable morning! If he only knew, she thought wildly, and then composed herself to reply quietly, "It was most interesting, *señor*. And you?"

Luis paused, two stairs up, arrested by her conventional response. "I enjoy riding," he said after a moment's consideration. "You must try it while you are here. Esteban keeps a good stable." And without giving her a chance to make any further comment, he mounted the rest of the stairs two at a time.

Caroline sauntered across the hall, unsure of what to do or where to go. The salon where Doña Isabel had accosted her earlier was empty, and breathing a little more freely, she moved across to the windows.

From here it was possible to see the forecourt and the sweep of formal gardens away to the left. Within the high walls of the fortresslike building were manicured lawns and flower beds and a carefully pruned row of fruit trees espaliered against the stone, softening its grim exterior. A means of escape, reflected Caroline dryly, turning as footsteps sounded behind her.

"There you are, Miss Leyton." Her employer stood framed in the arch of the open doorway, correct and businesslike in his pale gray attire. Aside from the fact that he was smaller than his brother, and stockier, his features were not as finely chiseled, and his tongue appeared to moisten his thick lips as he took in the delightful picture Caroline made. Silhouetted by the sun, her hair was like a pale aureole around her head, and he held out his hand encouragingly, urging her to join him. "Lunch is an informal meal at San Luis, *señorita*," he added gently. "I will show you how we help ourselves."

Taking a deep breath, Caroline crossed the salon again to join him, and his hand lightly cupped her elbow. "I hope you had no trouble with Emilia after I left, *señorita*?" he inquired as they passed through the hall.

Caroline squashed the desire to release herself from his grasp and assured him that his daughter had been an exemplary pupil.

"This is good," he exclaimed, obviously pleased. "For too long she has had no kind of discipline. I hope you will understand me when I say that I expect your support in all things, and—" he paused, fingering his tie "—trust that you will remember it is I, and no one else, who gives you your instructions."

His meaning was unmistakable, and Caroline's lips tightened. "Of course, *señor*," she murmured, stifling her protests, and her employer permitted a self-satisfied smile.

Esteban escorted her to the morning room. It was not the room where they had eaten the night before and was much less ornate than most of the rooms in the hacienda. Exquisitely embroidered turquoise-and-gold tapestries took the place of elaborate paneling, making the room light and airy. Now long French windows had been opened onto a sunlit terrace where an arched colonnade provided shade for long buffet tables, and Caroline could not suppress the gasp of pleasure that escaped her when she saw the dappled waters beyond. A patio, checkered with mosaics, surrounded the sunken pool, and a realistically poised jaguar was frozen in an attitude of menace, a crystal-clear fountain cascading from its jaws.

"The Patio del Jaguar!" announced Esteban with a

flourish. "A fitting background for the lion of San Luis, would you not agree?" he prompted.

Caroline, slightly disconcerted by this display of conceit, hid her misgivings in a projected show of admiration. "The jaguar," she murmured effusively, "he looks so real!" And she escaped his oppressive possession by stepping down into the brilliant sunshine.

Until then she had not appreciated how hot it really was. The thick walls of the hacienda provided their own brand of air conditioning, and until she felt the sun beating down on her head, she had felt reasonably cool. Now she lifted her face almost worshipfully to the sun, pressing her hands to the back of her neck. It was a gesture of unconscious sensuality, but she was unaware of it until her attention was caught by a movement at an upper window. Almost against her will, her eyes were locked for a brief moment with Luis's, and then he drew back out of sight and she was left with the awareness of Don Esteban's brooding appraisal. Immediately her hands dropped to her sides, and relinquishing her desire to explore further, she returned to the terrace.

"You are a sun worshiper, Miss Leyton?" Esteban inquired, his voice thicker than she remembered it.

She forced a light smile. "I—I didn't realize it was so hot," she confessed. "What a pity one can't swim in the pool."

"That could be arranged," Esteban remarked huskily, his eyes lingering on the burgeoning curve of her breast, but Caroline chose to ignore him as she turned determinedly to the buffet tables.

A mouth-watering display of dishes awaited their attention. Various salads and their attendant sauces flanked curried eggs and creamy stuffed avocados, shellfish served in their own shells, cold meats and gelatines, and chilled fruit juices. For the more adventurous there were steaming enchiladas and tacos, dishes of fried chicken, bowls of chili con carne that Caroline knew from experience was nothing like the chili she'd had at home, and delicious caramel desserts nestled in beds of fresh peaches and apricots.

Esteban encouraged her to try the tortillas, but Caroline chose a chicken salad. She was seated on the terrace, a glass of chilled white wine in her hand, when Luis and Emilia joined them.

"Ah, *chica*," exclaimed Esteban, beckoning his daughter toward him, apparently having forgotten his attitude toward her earlier. Wary of his uncertain temper, the child approached.

Someone had washed her face and brushed her long dark hair, and the frilly white dress had been replaced by an equally unsuitable pink one with long lace sleeves that, Caroline suspected must be quite uncomfortable in the heat. A slight bruise on her cheekbone was all that remained of the blow her father had delivered earlier, but Caroline guessed it was tender, and she flinched when Esteban flicked it with a careless finger.

"Let that be a lesson to you, Emilia," he admonished the child lightly. "You are to do exactly as Miss Leyton tells you, and I expect to hear that she has no further trouble with you."

"Yes, *señor*." Emilia glanced at Caroline from beneath her dark lashes, and glimpsing the rekindled hostility, Caroline wished her employer would have chosen less ambiguous words. Did Emilia think she had been complaining about her? Or did the child imagine she had told him of her previous insolence? Either way it was going to be a continuous struggle keeping Emilia and her father on good terms, and she didn't honestly know if she wanted that responsibility. Then she encountered Luis's gray gaze and knew that, for good or ill, she was already committed—although to what, she had yet to discover.

Aside from the inherent disharmony among the participants, it was very pleasant eating lunch on the terrace. The sun filtering through the flowering vine cast moving shadows over the mellow stonework, and the shrubs spilling from their tubs around the pool dappled the monolithic stillness of the crouching predator. Insects buzzed among the flame trees and exotically patterned butterflies skimmed the falling, bubbling fountain, adding the frantic flutter of their wings to the cooling effluence of the water.

Esteban was disposed to be affable, and although Luis entered the conversation only rarely, those occasions when his brother addressed him were not the fraught offensives of the night before. On the contrary, the two men discussed the estate and its problems, and if sometimes Esteban's contempt for his brother's more democratic methods of running the hacienda surfaced, he quickly disguised it behind a mask of urbanity. Perhaps he wanted to show that he could be tolerant, too, Caroline reflected, tense in spite of herself when Luis chose to argue.

Emilia, after attracting her father's initial attention, took no part in the conversation at all, spending her time feeding small pieces of bread to the white doves that flew down from the cupola above their heads. She was evidently accustomed to her father's variable moods, and Caroline felt a sudden sympathy for her. It could not be easy, living here without friends or companions, and she determined to try to show the child how to play as well as work.

The meal over, a black-clad nursemaid appeared to take Emilia away for her siesta, and taking the opportunity presented when one of Esteban's servants came to speak to him, Caroline, too, made her escape. She needed time to herself, she decided, time to assimilate her experiences here so far, and with a feeling of weariness out of all proportion to the amount of work she had accomplished, she made her way up to her room.

With the blinds drawn it was very cool and pleasant lying on her bed, and she relaxed almost immediately. Perhaps it was not going to be as bad as she had first thought, she thought sleepily, losing consciousness before her brain had time to examine the things she had learned.

She awakened a couple of hours later, feeling considerably refreshed. When she released the blinds she saw that the shadows were longer, and in the distance the sea had a distinctly amber tinge. She longed to be near the sea, to plunge into its cool waters and dispel the sticky aftermath of her nap, but as that was not possible, she took a shower.

Afterward she dressed in cream cotton pants and a loose embroidered smock with wide elbow-length sleeves. She would have preferred to wear a brief cotton top, leaving her slim arms bare, but the outfit seemed too immodest in the confines of the hacienda. Besides, she had no desire to give Don Esteban the wrong impression. After brushing her hair and reapplying light makeup, she left her room in search of a cool drink.

The hacienda seemed very quiet as she made her way downstairs, her sandaled feet echoing hollowly as she crossed the wide tiled hall. There was no one in either of the salons she entered, and the library was equally deserted, the French windows in the morning room closed now, the buffet tables removed. She was hesitating over whether to summon one of the servants when the door to a small anteroom she had noticed earlier opened and Luis Montejo appeared. He seemed deep in thought, his head bent and his dark brows drawn closely together, but when he saw her he put his hands in his pockets, regarding her presence with polite but distant inquiry.

"*Señorita*," he observed courteously, inclining his head. "Are you looking for my brother or Emilia? I should tell you that Esteban is resting and would not welcome being disturbed, and Emilia does not take lessons in the afternoon."

Caroline pressed her lips together. "As...as a matter of fact, I was hoping I might be able to get a glass of cold water. Consuella advised me not to drink the water from the taps upstairs."

"She was correct." Luis frowned. "In any case, the tanks become warm and the water is unpleasantly tepid. However—" he paused "—you may have something more appetizing if you prefer. There is a refrigerated cabinet in Esteban's study, containing various kinds of fruit drinks. Perhaps you would like one of them instead of cold water."

Caroline hesitated. "But won't your brother—"

"Esteban will never notice," Luis assured her with a curious twist of his mouth, leading the way along a corridor similar to the one upstairs. Only this time the portraits were interspersed with narrow fluted-glass windows, and the carpet underfoot was in shades of red and silver.

Esteban had not shown her his study during their morning tour, but now Luis led the way into a room only slightly smaller than the library. As in the library, there were shelves of files and books—mostly agricultural tomes, she noticed—and an imposing square desk set with two dark green telephones. The desk was neat and tidy, however, with no outstanding piles of papers awaiting attention, and Caroline decided that Esteban was either extremely efficient or extremely bored.

She chose a lime-juice cordial from the liquor cabinet, and then arched her brows when Luis took nothing. "Won't you join me?" she murmured, loath to be left to her own devices again. But the tall dark Mexican shook his head.

"I regret I do not have the time, *señorita*," he demurred politely, following her out of the room and closing the door. "But I have no doubt Esteban would not object if you chose to walk in the gardens, or borrowed one of the books from the library."

Caroline looked up at him mutinously, making no effort to open the ring-pull can. "I wanted to talk to you," she exclaimed, stung by his indifference, and his expression hardened as he met her resentful eyes.

"I am sure that if you have any questions my brother will be happy to answer them," he said, hooking his thumbs into his belt. "I hear that he approves of your behavior so far, and I am sure Emilia can only benefit from your example."

Caroline pursed her lips. "I don't want to talk to Don Esteban," she declared in a low tone. "I want to talk to you. I—I wanted to apologize for what happened—"

"There is no need," he interrupted her harshly, waving away her attempt at conciliation. "I am glad to have been of service, *señorita*. And now I have work to attend to."

Caroline heaved a sigh. Then before he could take too many steps away from her, she hastened after him. "¡*Señor! Señor*, you said I might be able to ride while I was here: could I do so now? Emilia doesn't need me, as you said, and I'm not in the mood for reading."

Luis's lean dark face was intent. "*Señorita*, you cannot ride alone. Surely you realize that. Aside from the evident dangers, a woman does not go out unescorted. I suggest you discuss the matter with my brother and ascertain his opinion."

Caroline gazed up at him frustratedly, brushing back her hair with an impatient hand. "You mean—I'm a prisoner here, is that it? I'm not allowed outside the hacienda without a prison escort!"

"You are overdramatizing the situation, *señorita*," Luis exclaimed heavily, glancing around him as if hoping for a distraction. "I am sure that something will be arranged if you request it. Who knows, maybe *el patrón* himself will accompany you. Even though it may result in having to ride in the carriage."

"The carriage?" Caroline echoed blankly, and Luis sighed.

"My brother does not ride, *señorita*," he retorted flatly. "But he may be persuaded to make an exception in your case."

Caroline caught her lower lip between her teeth, biting hard. "I don't want your brother to escort me," she burst out impetuously. "And if you won't take me, then I shall find some way to go alone—"

"You will not!" he overrode her declaration with harsh admonition. "Be assured, *señorita*, I shall inform Esteban if you do attempt to do so, and it may very well result in your forfeiting any opportunity in the future."

Caroline gasped. "You'd do that?" She shook her head. "You brought me here. Doesn't that give you any sense of responsibility at all?"

"I did not bring you here, *señorita*," he contradicted her forcefully. "I transported you the few miles from Las Estadas, that is all. *You* applied for this job, *you* accepted the appointment and *you* traveled all these miles, at the instigation of Señora Garcia, to take up the position. How can you blame me if it is not wholly to your liking?"

Looking into his grim face, Caroline wondered how she had had the nerve to say what she had. But it was said now, and she could not retract it. So she stood her ground, facing him a little uncertainly and summoning her courage to go on.

"But you didn't warn me what to expect, did you?" she accused him recklessly. "You didn't tell me that your brother liked inflicting pain, or that your aunt was likely to insult me—"

"Doña Isabel insulted you? How did she do that?"

Caroline shook her head. "She...she accused me of being one of...one of your father's—"

"I understand." Luis held up his hand to silence her, his face twisting impatiently. "Did you tell Esteban?"

"He knew," said Caroline dully, feeling a headache beginning to probe at her temples. "He was there."

She sighed. "Oh, what does it matter? You don't really care about me. Just so long as Emilia doesn't suffer."

Luis watched her as she walked away from him, her head bent, her silky hair falling at either side of her face, exposing the vulnerable nape of her neck. Then he said a word that was as coarse as any his brother had used, before going after her.

"Tomorrow morning," he said harshly as he passed her, scarcely slowing his stride. "At six o'clock, *señorita*. I shall be waiting in the hall."

CHAPTER FOUR

PERHAPS because she had slept during the heat of the day, Caroline found it hard to sleep that night. Although her room was dark and cool, her thoughts were hot and excited, and she tossed around restlessly on the softly sprung mattress, unable to find a comfortable place to relax. Even without the restriction of the sheet her skin felt moist and prickly, and her heart seemed to be beating unnaturally loud.

She determinedly turned her mind to thoughts of home, realizing that, apart from a card from Mérida, she had not yet written to her parents. Tomorrow she would have to try to find the time to compose a letter, and hope that the strangeness of her surroundings would not be discernible from her descriptions. In spite of her own misgivings she didn't want her parents to worry, and her mother surely would if she suspected the truth of the situation at San Luis.

It was harder to think of Andrew, but she did, realizing with a pang that she had scarcely thought of him all day. His image had receded, to be replaced by a darker, harder profile with the long straight nose and finely molded lips of the ascetic. Luis de Montejo! A man different from other men, yet just as disturbing to her peace of mind.

Thrusting aside his image, she recalled Don Esteban's conversation that evening. Luis had not joined them for dinner, but Doña Isabel had, and Caroline had been uneasy until it became apparent that the old lady was quite lucid. Dressed in the inevitable black, but with a fine lace mantilla draped around her shoulders and caught at the throat with an enormous diamond pin, she presided over the table with her nephew, occasionally subjecting Caroline to a not-unfriendly appraisal.

"Esteban tells me you are from London, *señorita*," she observed, her somewhat clawlike fingers crumbling the roll on her plate. "I went to London once. In 1946. I thought it was an ugly place, and it rained—all the time."

"Tía Isabel, London was subjected to saturation bombing during the war," Esteban inserted patiently. "What you saw was the result of that desecration. I myself have been there since, and I can assure you it is not ugly."

"Were you born in London, *señorita*?" Doña Isabel persisted, undaunted by her nephew's interruption.

Caroline shook her head. "My family lives just outside London, *señora*. In Buckinghamshire. But I attended university in London, and I know it very well."

"Hah!" Doña Isabel nodded. "And did your parents approve of this?"

Caroline frowned. "Approve of what, *señora*?"

"Approve of your attending the university, of course." Doña Isabel shook her head. "And traveling so far, without a duenna," she added. "When I was a girl such things would never have been permitted."

"Miss Leyton is a product of the twentieth century, *tía*," Don Esteban interposed smoothly. "And we should be grateful that she has chosen to come to San Luis and be the companion Emilia needs."

Doña Isabel pursed her lips. "Emilia needs a mother's care," she declared, nibbling at the tips of her fingers. "Brothers and sisters to bring her companionship." She sighed. "But with you a *viudo*, Esteban, and your brother destined for *la iglesia*, how can we hope for miracles?"

"I do not think Miss Leyton would agree with you," Esteban retorted now. "Emilia is not unique." He smiled at Caroline, his dark eyes warmly approving. "And with the *señorita*'s assistance, we may all prosper."

Caroline applied herself to the spicy mixture of rice and chicken on her plate, embarrassed by Don Esteban's unction, and Doña Isabel shrugged her thin shoulders in dismissal.

"Perhaps," she murmured without conviction, and to Caroline's relief the subject was dropped.

No one questioned where Luis was, but while they were taking coffee in the salon later his name entered the conversation. It was Doña Isabel who introduced the subject, and Caroline's cheeks burned during the old lady's disturbing exchange with her nephew.

"I saw that woman leaving the hacienda again this afternoon," she announced irritably, clattering the fragile coffee cup in its saucer. "I saw her leaving by the *puerta accesoria*. I will not have that woman in this house, Esteban! You must speak to Luis again!"

Her nephew looked slightly disconcerted by this unprovoked outburst, and his words in consequence were persuasively appeasing. "Tía Isabel, *cara*, I do not think we need discuss this affair in front of MIss Leyton. I will speak to Luis, as you say, and the matter will be dealt with."

"You have said that before, Esteban," declared Doña Isabel peevishly, not prepared to surrender so easily. "If Luis has need of a woman of that sort, why can he not arrange to meet her in the village?"

"Tía Isabel, I have told you, I will attend to it." Don Esteban's eyes glittered ominously. "What Luis chooses to do in his spare time is not Miss Leyton's concern, and I suggest you restrict your remarks to less personal matters."

Caroline, in truth, was at a loss to know what to think. Who was this woman Doña Isabel spoke about? Some penitent of Luis's, here for him to hear her confession? Some poor creature dependent on him for charity? Or, more realistically, judging from the censure in Doña Isabel's voice, the kind of woman used for only one purpose, the idea of which caused a definitely hollow feeling in the pit of Caroline's stomach.

It was this as much as anything that was keeping her awake. She was disturbed by what she had heard, puzzled by the reasons behind it and by the awareness of her own involvement. Was this woman the one whom Luis had been with when she saw him that afternoon? Was she the reason for that thoughtful expression he had been wearing? And was she, Caroline, by her persistence, an unwitting accessory to his deception of his brother?

Eventually she slept, only to be awakened seemingly minutes later by an impatient tattoo on her door. Someone was knocking, determined to arouse her, and she struggled up on her pillows, groping for her watch.

It was six-fifteen and scarcely light outside, but her heart pounded in sudden comprehension. It was Luis. It had to be. And scrambling off the bed, she sped across the room to the door.

"Who is it?" she breathed, her throat dry, and the constant tapping ceased.

"Montejo," he said with grim inflection. "Have you changed your mind?"

"No! *no!*" Caroline spoke without hesitation, glancing behind her helplessly at the tumbled bed. "Can—can you give me ten minutes? I've overslept. I promise I won't be long."

"Five minutes," he declared, delivering one last blow to the panels, and she heard his booted feet as he strode away down the corridor.

She washed her face and cleaned her teeth, contenting herself with the briefest of ablutions, and dressed without deliberation in purple jeans and cotton shirt. She wore boots instead of shoes, folding the legs of her jeans inside them, and snatched up a sweater as she went out the door. She didn't bother with makeup. Her skin was naturally pink from the haste with which she had readied herself, and her hair swung silkily around her cheeks as she hurried along the lamplit corridor.

Luis was waiting in the hall. She saw him as soon as she reached the landing, pacing restlessly across the black-and-gold tiling, flicking his knee-length black boots with the long muzzle of a rifle. The gun gave her páuse. An unexpected weapon in the hands of an expert, she was sure, as lean and dangerous as the man himself. Dressed in black, he exuded a lethal magnetism, and she realized how uncomplicated her relationship with Andrew had been compared to the feelings this man evoked in her.

He saw her as she started to descend, and his gray eyes narrowed speculatively. She was made uncomfortably aware that he did not consider jeans suitable attire for riding, but his words to her were impersonal, negating his unspoken reprobation.

"We will need to hurry if you are to see anything of the estate," he said flatly, and without giving her time to reply he thrust open the door through which she had seen him entering the previous afternoon and indicated that she should precede him.

Caroline found herself in a small cloakroom with two more doors opening from it. The first was heavy and studded, with a crucifix nailed to is surface, but the other was the one Luis opened, giving access to the garden outside. Caroline licked her lips. This had to be the side door Doña Isabel had mentioned the night before. She had looked up *puerta accesoria* in her dictionary before going to bed, and she swallowed rather convulsively at the confirmation of the old lády's story, and the inevitable conclusions she had reached.

Outside the air was incredibly fresh and sweet, and for a moment she forgot her apprehensions. And then Luis closed the door behind them and bid her follow him. She hastened in his footsteps, aware of the sudden weight she felt upon her.

Luis had evidently made all the arrangements earlier, for his own mount and a soft-eyed chestnut mare were already saddled and waiting for them. The old Mexican stableman smiled benevolently as Luis took the time to thank him for his trouble, and proffered his hands for Caroline to use as a mounting block. After a brief glance at Luis Caroline accepted his assistance, and he hoisted her firmly onto the chestnut's back.

It was easily four years since Caroline had ridden a friend's pony on a farm near her home in Buckinghamshire, but the lessons she'd had then still stood her in good stead. The mare was much bigger than the pony had been, of course, but she was docile and amenable, and after assuring himself that Caroline could handle her, Luis swung himself onto the back of a dark red gelding. He tucked the butt of the rifle into a leather pocket attached to the front of his saddle and then said something in Spanish to the grinning old man.

"*Desde luego, señor*," he answered eagerly and hastened into the stables again, to reappear moments later with a wide-brimmed sombrero. "*Por usted, señorita*," he said, offering it to Caroline. Meeting Luis's eyes again, she made an involuntary little shrug as she took it.

"Never go riding without a hat," he advised her softly, and with a helpless gesture she jammed the well-worn crown onto her head.

"*Mucha suerte, señorita, señor*," exclaimed the old man cheerfully as they rode out of the yard, and Luis raised his hand in farewell as he urged the horses forward.

Gomez came out to open the gates for them, and Luis had a smile and a friendly word for him, too. Like the stableman, Gomez evidently liked the younger Montejo, and Caroline couldn't help wondering whether Esteban inspired the same affection in his employees.

Beyond the gates the ground sloped away steeply in a series of gullies and shallow ravines thick with shrubs and trailing creepers. The lush vegetation had a primitive beauty, but Caroline couldn't help remembering what Emilia had said about snakes and spiders, and she felt sure this was exactly the sort of habitat they would frequent. She was relieved therefore, when Luis did not ride down the track toward the village but branched off on a circular route that followed the walls of the hacienda for some way before giving naturally onto the gentler incline that formed the northern boundary.

Given her head, the mare was quite happy to follow Luis's mount's example and trotted obediently after the more spirited animal. But as the shrubby undergrowth gave way to open grassland, the gelding quickened its pace, and Caroline had to concentrate to keep her seat as the mare broke into a gallop. Yet it was stimulating after all the tensions of the past couple of days, and she was glad that the cord of her hat was under her chin when the wind caught the sombrero, tipping it behind her head.

She was breathless and exhilarated when Luis finally slowed his mount and the mare caught up with him, jostling its rider. Caroline's knee was pressed for a moment against Luis's booted ankle, and the color flowered in her cheeks as he propelled the mare away.

"You ride like someone bent on a course to disaster," he remarked dryly, just when she had been preparing herself for his approval. "Do you always let your mount run away with you like that? Or were you simply incapable of doing anything about it?"

Caroline gave him an indignant look. "I was in control," she exclaimed defensively, patting the mare's neck with a knowledgeable hand. "I'm sorry if our collision caused you some discomfort, but I wasn't aware your boots were so fragile!"

Luis's mouth drew down at the corners. "In this terrain one should always be in control," he retorted grimly, directing her attention to a spot some four hundred yards away. "Have you any idea how little time it takes for a herd of cattle to bear down on you, or the kind of injuries that can be sustained by so many plunging hooves?"

Caroline looked at the moving blur of darkness on the pale horizon. Until he pointed them out to her, she had been unaware of their presence, but now she quivered in the grip of her imagination. She had seen the frightening results of a stampede in films and on television, and she could certainly picture her terror if the herd turned this way. Even from her window they had seemed thick in number and slightly menacing, and to be this near to them was itself unnerving.

"I—I didn't know, I didn't realize," she said now in futile expiation. "What do we do now? Do we go back? I've never been this close to a herd of cattle before."

"I doubt you have," he conceded wryly, controlling the mettlesome gelding with the ease of long experience. "And no, we do not go back. We ride through them. So long as we do not startle them, there is no danger."

Caroline was not entirely convinced. The eyes she turned in Luis's direction mirrored her indecision, and his stiffness eased as he attempted to reassure her.

"Come," he said, urging his mount near to hers. Reaching out, he lifted the sombrero back onto her head. "We will walk the horses for a while. That way you can be sure we will disturb no one."

The sun, which had previously been sheltering behind a bank of clouds, cleared suddenly and spread fingers of rose pink and palest orange over the plain. Caroline could hear the birds squawking as they swooped overhead, and as she paced the mare beside the gelding she had time to look around her and enjoy the increasing warmth. She had tied the sleeves of her sweater around her shoulders, but she pulled it off now and fastened it to the front of her saddle. She rolled the sleeves of her shirt back to the elbows, exposing her slim arms to the sun, and then felt slightly chastened when Luis looked her way. Even in his black pants and leather jerkin he did not seem to be bothered by the sun as she was, but he refrained from making any comment, and she determined not to let his attitude influence her.

"How far away is the sea?" she asked, shading her eyes and endeavoring to ignore their approach to the herd.

Luis gave the matter some consideration. "As the

crow flies, some ten miles," he replied briefly, and Caroline gasped in surprise.

"So far?" she exclaimed, steering the mare around a clump of marsh grasses. "But I thought—I mean—it seemed so near from the window of my room."

"Distances can be deceptive," remarked Luis carelessly, narrowing his eyes against the glare. "Particularly when the ground is flat. Why?" He glanced sideways at her. "Were you planning to dip your toes in the Gulf of Mexico?" He shook his head. "I regret you will have to save that doubtful privilege until Esteban chooses to take you in the Rover."

Caroline sighed. "I just thought it might have been nice to take Emilia to the beach," she averred, avoiding his eyes. "But if we have to go by road, I suppose I could take her myself. I can drive."

Luis gave her a wry look. "Do you really think Esteban will let you take Emilia out without his escort?" He shrugged. "I think not."

Caroline made an impatient gesture. "Because I'm a woman alone? Oh, this is ridiculous!"

Luis made no response, and she expelled her breath with evident frustration. "Do you mean to tell me that even in a car we have to have a bodyguard?"

"If it pleases you to call it that, then yes," Luis inclined his head. "In any case, as far as Emilia is concerned, there is always the danger of kidnapping, a common enough occurrence in these times. You would not wish to put her life in danger."

Caroline pressed her lips together. "No. No, of course not."

"Good." Luis made a dismissing gesture. "So you will do as Esteban says, *no es verdad*?"

Caroline moved her shoulders slightly resentfully, but she voiced no protest as Luis took possession of the mare's bridle to lead it through the grazing ranks of cattle.

Some of the beasts raised their heads to watch their progress, staring with wide brooding eyes, but as Luis had said, they were not aggressive. On the outer flanks of the herd the pair came upon several of the gauchos whose job it was to guard the cattle, and they called greetings to Luis from their lazy bivouac beneath a clump of stunted cedars. They had lighted a fire to make breakfast, and the scent of coffee was appetizing, mingling with the inevitable smell of beans and of the thin corn pancakes that were their staple diet. They offered to share their repast with the patron and his lady, but although Caroline expected him to accept, Luis refused their generosity with formal politeness.

"I should not care for you to suffer some unfortunate stomach upset because of my carelessness," he told her flatly as they put some distance between them and the drovers. "The men are kind but not always scrupulous, and you are not immune to infection."

"You mean, if you had been alone you would have accepted their invitation?" Caroline asked, glancing back over her shoulder. Luis shrugged. "Perhaps. It is of no matter." He urged his horse forward. "Come. We will ride for some way along the bank of the river before we have to turn back."

"Turn back?"

The consternation in Caroline's voice was unmistakable, but Luis only nodded. "It is after seven, *señorita*," he pointed out patiently, showing her the face of the slim gold watch on his wrist. "And it will take us the better part of an hour to get back. You would not wish to be late for your lessons with Emilia, would you?"

Caroline supposed he was right, but she was disappointed that the time had passed so quickly, almost without her realizing it. She had wanted to talk to him, really talk to him, to get to know him better; and perhaps to discover for herself the real truth behind Esteban's assertions concerning Luis's mother. But now he was talking of turning back, and she had no idea when she might get another chance to be alone with him like this.

They cantered across a marshy expanse of ground to where the somewhat muddy waters of the river surged forcefully downstream. Close at hand she could see that the river had been swollen by the storms of two days before, and whereas from her window she had seen only the trees and shrubs that grew on the higher ground, now she saw the torn-off branches of trees and other debris being swept irresistibly toward the ocean. Once the inflated carcass of some animal, trapped by the powerful undercurrent, swept by them, and Caroline shivered at the realization of how little chance of survival anything would have caught in that pitiless flow.

"My father drained this land," remarked Luis, pulling the gelding's head around and compelling the animal along the bank. "He deepened the channel of the river and used the silt to raise the level of the ground. It greatly increased the value of his holding."

"I can imagine." Caroline urged the mare alongside him, looking down into the swirling waters. "Have you lived here all your life, *señor*? Or did you, like your brother, attend school in England?"

Luis glanced her way broodingly, his brief spate of cordiality disappearing. "I am sure the details of my education can be of no interest to you, *señorita*," he essayed without enthusiasm. "Shall we ride to the ridge before turning back?"

"Your brother told me a little about your father when he showed me around the house," Caroline persisted, shifting in the saddle. "We talked about your family. It was very interesting. He explained that you're really half brothers, and that although you had the same father, you had different mothers—"

"*¡Basta!*" Luis's lean face darkened with sudden anger, and he overrode her submission with grim determination. "To what purpose do you tell me this, *señorita*?" he demanded. "Of what possible interest could Esteban's confidences be to me?"

Caroline flushed. "I was . . . simply making conversation, that's all," she defended herself stiffly. "You mentioned your father, and I—I reciprocated. I'm sorry. I didn't know the subject was taboo!"

Luis massaged the muscles at the back of his neck with an impatient hand, the action parting the lapels of his sleeveless jerkin, exposing the straining buttons of his dark shirt. "It is not taboo, *señorita*," he told her at last, expelling his breath with heavy emphasis. "But do not take me for a fool, either, whatever Esteban has said."

Caroline was confused and embarrassed now, but somehow she had to remain composed. "I don't know what you think your brother has said, *señor*," she declared, taking the offensive. "He spoke about the history of the house and explained some of the legends associated with the area. And...and as far as your family is concerned, he he merely defined the situation."

"Indeed." Luis's expression was skeptical now, his mouth oddly twisted, his attitude one of veiled contempt. "You expect me to believe that? You did not then hope to provoke me into contradicting Esteban?"

"Contradicting him?" Caroline's face burned in spite of herself. "No, I—"

"Oh, let us have done with this," Luis interrupted harshly. "I know my brother, *señorita*. I know what he is capable of. I know what he must have told you. But I have no intention of satisfying your squalid curiosity by compounding his deficiency. Do I make myself clear?" His lips curled. "And if that is the real reason behind this sudden desire for horseback riding, then I regret that you have wasted your time!"

"You flatter yourself, *señor*." Caroline caught her breath. "I was looking forward to this outing. I was looking forward to getting away from the hacienda. Believe it or not, I have ridden before, and I have always enjoyed it. Accepting your company was just a means to an end, as it seems I am not allowed the freedom here I've been used to. I didn't ask for your brother's confidences and I wouldn't presume to expect yours." She drew another trembling breath and adjusted the strap of her sombrero before adding, unforgivably, "But in one respect, I would agree with Don Esteban. You are jealous of him. As jealous as hell! And that's why you're so damned touchy when your brother's name is mentioned!"

It was a damning indictment, and although Caroline told herself it had been justified, she felt terribly guilty as she sat there waiting for his denouncement.

But it never came. With an indifferent shrug of his shoulders Luis dug his knees into the gelding's sides, and the animal obediently broke into a canter. Within seconds he was some distance ahead of her, widening the gap with every strike, and with a feeling of helpless compliance Caroline was obliged to follow him.

The ridge he had mentioned was some half a mile away, a curving bluff of limestone forming a natural ravine, at the bottom of which the river tumbled in contracted fury. Luis had reined his mount at the edge of the cliff, and Caroline rode up to him reluctantly, hanging some way back, aware that—as far as he was concerned, at least—she had destroyed any hope of an amicable relationship between them.

When he turned his head to look at her she had to steel herself not to glance away, and then her heart lurched with sudden palpitation when she saw that he was smiling. He sat there, one arm resting lazily across the pommel of his saddle, his expression wry and slightly mocking, and she knew without a shadow of a doubt that no matter what Esteban said, jealousy was not the reason for Luis's behavior.

"Feeling better?" he inquired as she nudged her mare nearer to him. Caroline made a gesture of defeat.

"I'm sorry," she said, pushing back the hat and shaking her hair free. "I was rude, and I'm sorry." She looked at him ruefully. "Will you forgive me?"

"There is nothing to forgive," Luis retorted, straightening in the saddle. "You have your opinions, and you are right to voice them. I am simply not used to such candor."

Caroline sighed. "I shouldn't have said what I did," she declared, shaking her head, and then swung herself down from the saddle to walk tentatively to the rim of the ravine. "Would you believe me if I said I didn't mean it?"

"I would advise you not to go too near the edge," Luis commented dryly. When she paid him no heed, he, too, dismounted and, flexing his muscles, came to stand beside her.

Caroline was intensely aware of him, of the lean length of his thigh only inches from hers, and of the fact that she had only to stretch her fingers to touch him. But she was aware, too, of the precariousness of their relationship, and while she didn't want to do or say anything to disrupt it yet again, she had to relieve her own sense of inadequacy.

"Do you believe me?" she probed, looking up at him and feeling her breathing constrict when the intentness of his gray gaze locked with hers.

"What does it matter to you?" he asked, his voice taut with suppressed emotion. "I shall be leaving here the day after tomorrow, *señorita*. My opinion is not important. It is with my brother you will have to deal." He paused then, looking away from her to follow the plunging course of the river. "But it may be that you are right," he added with some self-derision. "Perhaps I am jealous of Esteban. Oh, yes—" as she started to protest "—perhaps I am. But not, I fear, for the reason you imagine."

"What do you mean?"

Caroline spoke huskily, but Luis had already turned away from her, adjusting the stirrup leathers hanging from his saddle before thrusting his foot into the iron stirrups.

"Can you not guess?" he asked, settling himself more comfortably in the saddle. Her eyes widened as she gazed up at him. "Never imagine a priest is not a man, *señorita*," he concluded, causing her lips to part in confusion. "Particularly a priest who is not yet ordained." He grimaced. "In spite of my maternal heritage, I find that ultimately I am still my father's offspring."

Caroline was bewildered. "Your maternal heritage, *señor*? I—I don't understand—"

Luis bent his head as if it were suddenly too heavy for his neck to support, and looked down at her in resignation. "My mother lives at the Convent of the Sisters of the Annunciation, *señorita*. When my father died she took refuge there, and it is my brother's wish that I should follow her example."

CHAPTER FIVE

DON ESTEBAN had guests for dinner that evening.

They were a Señor and Señora Calveiro, from the neighboring estate of Los Calvados, and their daughter, Josetta. Caroline, who had been informed of the invitation at lunch, had hoped to be allowed to take dinner alone in her room, but Don Esteban would not hear of it.

"Luis will be joining us, of course," he said, spearing her with his dark gaze, and she wondered whether her unannounced outing with his brother had been reported to him. "I shall expect you to make up the numbers, *señorita*, and I am sure the Calveiros will wish to compliment me on my good fortune."

"You're very kind, *señor*."

Caroline had answered politely enough, but inside she had dreaded the evening ahead and the inevitable association with his brother. After that disturbing exchange on the ridge, they had ridden back to the house without any further opportunity for conversation, and once there, Luis had speedily excused himself from her presence. She had suspected he was already regretting his earlier frankness, and she doubted he would welcome an evening spent in the company of a confessor. She had been responsible, of course; it was all her fault. And her own feelings were so confused, the last thing she wanted was to make the situation any harder—for either of them.

But she had had little time to reflect on these thoughts. The arrival of the maid with her breakfast tray had interrupted the hasty shower she was taking, and afterward, dressed neatly in a navy shirt and skirt, she had found Emilia already in the library awaiting her.

The little girl had evidently decided the easier course was to obey her father, and Caroline was glad she had had the foresight to prepare the next day's lesson the previous morning while Emilia was writing an essay. In future she would have to find time to prepare their lessons on a more regulated basis, devoting different days to different subjects, but for the present she concentrated on keeping the child busy and interested. Mexican history had never been Caroline's strong point, but now she found herself reading about the Spanish invasion, the subsequent religious conversion and, ultimately, the mingling of Spanish and Indian blood to produce the mestizo race that presently predominated. She studied the campaigns of Benito Juárez and Porfirio Díaz, the latter dictatorship primarily responsible for the flourishing wealth of the hacenderos, and the revolution of 1910 that made such a hero of Pancho Villa, and realized how limited her knowledge had been up to that time. The more she learned, however, the more she was fascinated, and she refused to acknowledge that she was in any way influenced by her involuntary involvement with Luis.

Lunch was again a buffet meal, and for once Caroline was glad of Doña Isabel's presence to divert Esteban's attention from herself. Nevertheless the dark-eyed *patrón* of San Luis found plenty of occasions to bring her into the conversation, and she was made increasingly aware that little went on that he did not know about.

And yet, although there were several occasions when she had an opportunity to tell him that she had been riding with Luis, somehow she never seemed to find the right words. It didn't occur to her that his brother might have told him. Instinctively she guessed that Luis would leave it to her to make that decision, but the idea of telling Esteban, of laying herself open to his mockery and possible contempt, promoted only constraint, and she escaped after the meal feeling distinctly cowardly.

As on the previous afternoon, she sought the refuge of her own room and fell asleep on her bed. She had intended to prepare the following day's lessons for Emilia and to write to her mother, but exhaustion overtook her and she knew nothing more until the sun was rapidly sinking into the west.

She got off the bed reluctantly, aware of the approaching dinner party, and spent several minutes gazing at her reflection with critical eyes. The rest had left a slumberous languor about her, and there were faintly bruised shadows on her eyelids. She had slept too soundly, she decided, refusing to acknowledge their significance, and dismissed the uneasy realization that the last thing she had thought of was Luis's face when he told her he was his father's son. Unbidden, Doña Isabel's words came back to her, the old lady's angry denunciation of the woman she had seen in the hacienda. All of a sudden it did not seem so incredible that there was some female in Luis's life, and Caroline perceived her own reactions to the fact with a sense of impatience.

Leaving the bedroom, she stripped off her clothes and took a cold shower, reveling in the brisk spray, dispersing the lingering threads of lassitude. It would not do to face her employer without being fully alert, she reflected dryly, and while she might resent his arbitrary use of her presence, he was her employer and she felt obliged to accommodate him.

She took the only black dress she possessed out of the wardrobe and flung it onto the bed, studying its simple lines without enthusiasm. Made of a synthetic fibre that combined the uncrushableness of polyester with the softness of silk, she had bought it to attend a cocktail party with Andrew, and the memories it evoked were not welcome.

It had been one of those professorial gatherings beloved of the lecturing fraternity, just after Caroline had taken her final exams. Tricia, Andrew's wife, was ill again, some complication after another of her nervous upsets, and Andrew had cast caution to the winds and invited Caroline to join him. There had been some eyebrows raised at the sight of the handsome young professor escorting his erstwhile student, Caroline remembered ruefully, fingering the soft black folds. In spite of her father's position as a lecturer, their relationship was untenable. Andrew was a married man, and when Caroline encountered Tricia on the campus the following week, her unvoiced understanding had left Caroline feeling like a bitch. It was then that she'd begun to see the futility of her love for Andrew. He was never going to divorce Tricia; her father, the dean, would see to that. And because Caroline's own father was also prominent on campus, there seemed only one alternative.

With a sigh Caroline slipped the dress over her head and acknowledged without conceit that its darkness complemented her extreme fairness, for the sun had only tinted the pale contours of her face. Against the somber fabric her hair had the sheen of silver. The halter neckline exposed most of her neck and shoulders and the downy hollow of her back, but she couldn't help it. It was the most suitable thing she possessed, and she had seen many more provocative garments at the hotel in Mérida.

Dinner was at eight, but Don Esteban had asked her to join him for a predinner apertif at seven-thirty. It was a little after that time when Caroline left her room, and she was walking with her usual haste along the gloomy corridor when a door to her right suddenly opened. She was so shocked, she faltered in her stride, for she had supposed herself the only occupant of this wing. But Luis's unexpected appearance disabused her of that belief. She gazed at him speechlessly for a few moments before recovering her equilibrium.

"I am sorry. Did I startle you?" he inquired, emerging from the room and closing the door. She expelled her breath with feeling.

He was formally dressed this evening in a wine-colored, velvet evening suit, the matching silk of his shirt enhanced by a froth of lace. On many men, she realized, the extravagance would have looked feminine, but with Luis's hard features no such comparison was necessary. The shoulders beneath the soft pile of his jacket were broad and unpadded, the thighs molding the material like a second skin were powerful and muscular, and she knew from experience that with his sinewy strength, he had all the resourcefulness of a predator.

"I didn't—I didn't know your rooms were on this corridor," she admitted as he fell into step beside her. "It—it always seems so empty."

"They are not," Luis disillusioned her politely. "I have been visiting Tía Isabel, that is all. It is she, and not I, who shares this wing with you."

"Oh!" Caroline was aware of a sudden empty feeling, not wholly due to a sense of disappointment. Of all the occupants of the hacienda, Doña Isabel was the last person she would have chosen to share her seclusion. A feathering of goose bumps rippled her flesh.

"She is harmless, you know," Luis remarked quietly, as if aware of her apprehension, and Caroline glanced quickly at him. His perception where she was concerned was quite remarkable, but in this instance his reassurance was not convincing.

"When she is lucid," she retorted as they reached the head of the stairs, and preceded him down them before he could make any further comment.

Don Esteban's guests had arrived and were talking with him in the main salon, an imposing room with many fine pictures and furniture from the period of the last emperor. It was not the room that held Caroline's attention this evening, however, but the four men and women who awaited her there. Her mouth went dry when she encountered their critical gaze.

She had been right to wear black, she acknowledged flatly, but that was her only merit. The gowns of the two women who stood with Don Esteban bore no resemblance to hers, and their hostility was evident in every word and gesture. From the protection afforded by severely collared dresses with long buttoned sleeves, they looked down their thin noses at the outrageous English girl, subjecting her to their censure and unveiled disapproval.

To Caroline's dismay, Luis seemed amused by this display of self-righteousness, and it was left to Don Esteban to rescue the situation. Unlike his guests, he obviously found Caroline's appearance stunning, and he came toward her purposefully, possessing himself of her hand.

"You look—magnificent, *señorita*," he informed her gallantly, raising her fingers to his lips. Then he glanced around at the Calveiros and made a bow. "What a fortunate man I am to have three such beautiful women at my table!"

The introductions were brief, to Caroline's relief, and then Josetta Calveiro deserted her parents to move to Luis's side. Caroline heard her chattering away to him eagerly in their own language as she was appropriated by Don Esteban, and felt an unwelcome sense of resentment. It was obvious that Josetta was very young, and probably very immature, but did Luis have to behave as if he found her conversation absorbing?

"You are a stranger to Mexico, *señorita*," Señora Calveiro addressed her now. Caroline endeavored to concentrate on what she was saying.

"Oh, yes. Yes." She forced a faint smile. "I've never crossed the Atlantic before. It's an entirely new experience for me."

"And for Emilia, too, I am sure," endorsed Señora Calveiro through tight lips. "It must be quite enlightening for the child to be taught by someone who is obviously so...independent, Esteban. Beware she does not learn all the wrong things."

Esteban's thick lips parted as he selected another glass from the tray proffered by a hovering waiter. "Miss Leyton understands our situation here, Doña Julia," he affirmed, swallowing the lime-flavored cocktail without grace or hesitation, and taking another. "Besides, it is so good for Emilia to learn of the world outside San Luis." His fingers touched Caroline's in mute approval. "Who knows, we may all benefit from this young lady's arrival."

Señor Calveiro chose to intercede at that point, taking his host away to discuss some aspect of cattle raising, and Caroline was left to combat Señora Calveiro's animosity alone.

"You have made an ally of your employer, I perceive," the soberly garbed *matron* remarked coldly. "But have a care, *señorita*. Don Esteban has been the aspiration of many a hopeful intrigue, but to my knowledge he has never sought to repeat the mistakes of the past."

Caroline's fingers tightened on her glass as the woman's meaning became evident. "I can assure you, *señora*, I have no such aspirations," she responded politely. "My reasons for being here are precisely what they seem. I was employed, at the instigation of Don Esteban, by Señora Garcia; and if he finds my work satisfactory, then my purpose has been achieved."

Señora Calveiro frowned, regarding her daughter's continuing conversation with Luis with as little enthusiasm as Caroline. "I did not know that Juana's mother had any part in this," she murmured, almost absently. And then, returning her attention to the girl at her side, she added, "I am surprised Esteban permitted it."

"As Emilia's grandmother, surely Señora Garcia is entitled to the privilege," murmured Caroline awkwardly, not quite knowing how to answer her.

Señora Calveiro's eyes wandered again. "Perhaps," she murmured thoughtfully, tasting her cocktail as if it were bitter. "But after the scandalous way Juana treated Esteban, it is a measure of his tolerance that he permits any contact." She shrugged, arching her thin brows in an expression of inconsequence. "So long as the child is happy, I suppose we must all make allowances."

Caroline nodded, wishing desperately that someone would make allowances for her. With Esteban ensconced in conversation at the other side of the room, and Josetta monopolizing Luis, she was obliged to humor the elderly duenna, and it was becoming something of a strain.

Then she turned and found Luis's eyes upon her.

Until that instant she had not thought he was aware of her. Their conversation upstairs had given her no cause to think otherwise; he had not even complimented her on her appearance. But in that unguarded moment, when she intercepted his brooding gaze, she knew she had been mistaken, and she also knew that his interest in Josetta's chatter was no greater than hers in Señora Calveiro's.

Responding to the silent appeal in her eyes, Luis excused himself from the Mexican girl and crossed the richly woven pile of the carpet. His booted feet made little sound on the fabric, and the lithe resolution of his movements reminded Caroline of a feline. There was something intensely sensual in imagining the muscled hardness of his body beneath the yielding texture of his clothes; like the supple power of a jaguar beneath the deceptive softness of its skin.

"*Señora,*" he greeted Josetta's mother smoothly, returning his empty glass to the tray without taking another. "I trust Miss Leyton's presence has assured you that Emilia is in good hands."

"Miss Leyton has been telling me that Doña Elena made the arrangements," Señora Calveiro declared stiffly. "Without Esteban's good nature, where would we all be?"

"Where indeed?" murmured Luis politely, his thigh brushing Caroline's as he moved from one foot to the other. "Esteban should be an example to us all."

Caroline glanced at him swiftly as he spoke, expecting to see the mockery in his face, but he looked perfectly serious, and Señora Calveiro endorsed his trite statement. "I am pleased to hear you appreciate this, Luis," she said with less hostility than before. "I know your mother would agree with me when I say that you owe Esteban a lot, and not every brother is willing to forgive and forget."

"How succinctly you put it, *señora*," observed Luis with a smile that Caroline watched with blank disbelief. "I will give your good wishes to my mother the next time I see her, and you can be assured she will be interested to hear of your approval."

Surprisingly, this did not seem to meet with such a favorable reaction, and it was perhaps fortunate that a butler appeared at that moment to announce that dinner was served. Señora Calveiro immediately moved to join her husband and Esteban, and as Josetta was likewise engaged, for a few unguarded moments Caroline and Luis were alone.

"I would thank you for rescuing me if I knew what you were doing," she breathed, bending to deposit her half-empty glass on the low marble-topped table behind her. "I'm sorry. I didn't realize you were such an ardent sympathizer of your brother's. If I've said or done anything to offend you, please accept my apologies."

"Do not be foolish," Luis exhorted her roughly, his lean fingers curving around her wrist under cover of their bodies. "Would you have had me start an argument with her and arouse her sour suspicions? So far as Doña Julia is concerned, I am—how do you call it—the black sheep, and nothing I can say or do will alter her opinion."

"But why?" Caroline gazed at him, intensely aware of those strong fingers gripping her arm. His lips compressed impatiently, bracketing his mouth with harsh lines.

"Did not Esteban apprise you of the facts of Emilia's conception?" he demanded grimly. "Did he not divulge his heartache at his wife's indiscretions?"

"No!" Caroline moved her head negatively, and almost involuntarily his hand slid down to hers. She doubted he was as aware of their intimacy as she was, but her fingers parted to receive his probing ones.

"He will," said Luis now, his dark face taut with emotion.

Caroline's senses spun. "You mean. . . Emilia is your daughter?" she whispered, dreading his confirmation, and then caught her breath when his face convulsed.

"No!" he denied savagely, jerking her toward him so that for a pain-sweet moment she was close to his hard body. "Juana and I were never lovers. Emilia is not my daughter. Though why I should feel the need to defend myself to you, I do not know."

"No."

Caroline's response was choked but faint, and he looked down at her almost resentfully, his eyes smoldering with passion. "Oh, yes," he contradicted her at last, his mouth suddenly sensual. "Yes. I know. But there is nothing—*nothing*—I can do about it."

"And what is it you can do nothing about, *mi hermano*?" rasped another voice near Caroline's ear. They moved apart almost guiltily, Caroline thrusting her suddenly trembling hands behind her back. Esteban had come to join them, moving silently as his brother had done, and Caroline wondered agonizingly how long he had been standing there listening.

"I was merely confirming Señora Calveiro's opinion of you, Esteban," Luis assured him flatly, causing his brother's color to rise with unbecoming haste. "She is such a—how shall I put it—an admirer of yours, and I was confessing to Miss Leyton how—humble you make us all feel."

Esteban's mouth compressed. "You are not amusing, Luis," he countered coldly. "And Miss Leyton should know better than to listen to you." His hand reached purposefully for Caroline's elbow. "Come, *señorita*. You will sit with me during dinner, so that Señora Calveiro shall not think you take my brother's vows lightly."

Caroline's color rivaled his as they entered the dining room. She was aware of the Calveiros' eyes upon her, and of the almost brutal strength underlying the soft fingers gripping her arm. Most of all, she was aware of Luis's presence behind them and the disturbing connotations of Don Esteban's warning.

It was not an easy meal. Although she tried to concentrate on the food, Caroline's eyes were irresistibly drawn to the foot of the table where Luis was making conversation again with Josetta. What had he meant by the things he had said? What interpretation could she put upon his actions? And why should she feel so affected by it when she knew of the circumstances of his background?

"You find my brother's company appealing?" inquired her host under cover of the servants removing her scarcely touched plate of soup, and Caroline's wandering thoughts were speared.

"I beg your pardon?" she murmured, playing for time, shocked out of her reverie and unable to marshal her defenses.

Esteban's lips curved. "My brother," he repeated in a low voice, helping her to a generous portion of sliced chicken, served with rice and peppers and a rich strong-smelling sauce. Caroline's stomach revolted. "Don Luis. His attentions...flatter you, perhaps?"

Caroline moistened her dry lips. "He—I—I find his company...pleasant, yes," she conceded rather unevenly. "And please—no more." She held up unsteady fingers to the waiter. "I—I'm not very hungry."

"No?" Esteban looked sideways at her. "And why is that, señorita? Do you not find our menus tasteful? Or has my brother robbed you of what appetite you had?"

Caroline took a deep breath. "Don Esteban, your... your brother has said nothing to rob me of my appetite. I simply don't eat a lot, that's all." She determinedly dipped her fork into the rice on her plate and took a mouthful. "This is very nice. I—I like it."

Don Esteban shrugged his broad shoulders and applied himself to his food for a while, but just when

Caroline was beginning to breathe more easily he turned to her again.

"You may think I interfere," he said, causing her to look up at him with wide startled eyes. "But I know my brother better than you do, and it concerns me that you might. . . misinterpret his actions."

Caroline expelled her breath unevenly. "Honestly, *señor*—"

"No. I insist you listen to me, *señorita*." He frowned, concentrating for a moment on the food on his plate. Then he looked at her again. "I have told you, have I not, of our relationship?" And when Caroline permitted an uneasy nod, he continued, "What I have not told you, *señorita*, is that there is another reason why my brother and I can never be friends—"

"*Señor*—"

"He destroyed my marriage, *señorita*."

Caroline put down her fork and clasped her hands tightly together in her lap. She should have expected this, of course. After what Señora Calveiro had said, she should have known what was to come. What she could not accept was why Don Esteban should wish her to know this.

"I have shocked you," he said now, refilling his wineglass. "I am sorry." He swallowed some of the transparent liquid. "But you are young, *señorita*, and vulnerable, and I should not like you to be. . . hurt."

Caroline drew a deep breath. "Why are you telling me this, *señor*? Lu—Don Luis and I scarcely know each other. And. . . and as you pointed out, he will be returning to the seminary soon."

Esteban inclined his head. "Yet it comes to my notice that you have spent much time in his company during these past few days. Did you not go riding with him this morning? Or was it his village woman who accompanied him?"

Caroline's face flamed. "You must know it was me," she replied stiffly. "But—but it was at my instigation.

I—I wanted to see outside the gates of the hacienda. Don Luis offered to accompany me.''

"I see." Esteban studied the wine in his glass. "You did not think to ask me if you could ride beyond the gates of the hacienda?"

Caroline sighed. "I did think of it, yes—"

"But Luis was there, hm?"

"You were otherwise engaged, *señor*. Besides...I, well, Don Luis told me you did not ride."

"Ah!" Esteban swirled the wine around in its crystal container. "Luis told you that, did he?"

"Isn't it true?"

Caroline's question stemmed more from a desire to reassure herself that she had not been mistaken about Luis than from any real interest in Esteban's abilities. And as if aware of this, her host regarded her with mocking eyes.

"Let us say that, like all the things my brother will tell you, there is a grain of truth behind it, *señorita*," he replied. He bent his head. "But we have talked of Luis long enough. Come, tell me about Emilia. Has her education been neglected? Can you assure me that it is not beyond repair?"

This was easier ground, and in discussing his daughter's education Caroline found an almost painful relief. Despite the nuances in his comments concerning her predecessor, she was able to talk with confidence about Emilia's intelligence, and he was reluctantly impressed by the child's evident aptitude for study.

"So you think Emilia has the making of a scholar?" he remarked at last, draining his glass once again. "What a pity she is not one of your English misses, *señorita*. Who knows, maybe she, too, might have wished to assert her independence."

Caroline forced a faint smile, but she was aware that Don Esteban was drinking far more than anyone else at the table; and what was even more disturbing, Señora Calveiro and her daughter were watching them closely, as if she were to blame for his studied neglect of his other guests.

The meal dragged to its inevitable conclusion, and Caroline was heartily relieved when Don Esteban acknowledged the waiter's announcement that coffee had been prepared in the salon.

"Let me help you," he said, getting to his feet to draw back her chair, and she saw that despite the amount of wine he had consumed throughout the meal, he was still perfectly capable of supporting himself. It was she who stumbled as she rose, her haste to get away from the table overriding her attempt at composure. Don Esteban's fingers slid around her waist as he rescued her from her temporary loss of balance.

"No hurry, *señorita*," he murmured, his wine-scented breath fanning her cheek. A sense of revulsion out of all proportion to the incident sent a wave of heat through her body.

"Thank you. I can manage," she got out unevenly, drawing herself away from him, but not before she had seen the Calveiros exchange a significant glance that mirrored all too clearly their opinion of her behavior. What did they think she was, she wondered impotently, marching ahead of Don Esteban, flags of color burning in her cheeks. Were they so out of touch with everyday living that they imagined her only reason for coming here was to find a husband? Did they seriously believe she was interested in Don Esteban? Was it beyond the realms of the Calveiros' experience that a woman should want more from life than the security of a husband?

In the salon she sought the isolation of a satin-covered armchair, withdrawing herself mentally, if not physically, from the company. She accepted the cup of coffee proffered by an olive-skinned maid with trembling fingers, and then reviewed her position in the light of the present situation.

It seemed obvious she had made a mistake in coming here. Aside from feeling isolated because of the remoteness of the hacienda, she was being reluctantly drawn into the personal lives of her employers. It was useless to tell herself that it wasn't important, that she had a job to do and she should do it. She was involved, unwilling or otherwise; and what was more, her motives were being tried and judged by people who knew nothing about her, who lived in a society that was restricted by its own traditions.

"You seem...troubled," remarked a quiet voice beside her.

She looked up tensely into Luis's lean dark face. "I am," she said, in no mood to fence words with him. "I think I should not have come here."

Luis squatted down easily beside her, the soft material of his pants taut over the muscles of his thighs. "And what reason do you have for coming to this conclusion?" he inquired flatly. "Do not distress yourself on my account. I shall be leaving soon. You have nothing to fear from me."

Caroline caught her breath. "It—I—it has nothing to do with you," she exclaimed huskily. "I—I just feel a man would be more...suitable in this post."

Luis sighed. "So, what did Esteban say to you?"

"Don Esteban?" Caroline's tongue circled her lips. "Why—nothing."

Luis frowned. "So you had come to this decision before you came down to dinner?"

Caroline hesitated. "Not exactly."

"Then—"

"Oh, if you must know, I feel—I feel as if Señora Calveiro thinks I have...designs on your brother." She bent her head. "And I'm not sure he doesn't think that, also."

Luis shrugged, the gray eyes, almost on a level with hers, narrowed and speculative. "And why did you come, *señorita*?"

Caroline gasped. "You know why! Because I needed a job. Because it sounded...it sounded—"

"Exciting?"

"No. Interesting!" Caroline became aware that once again Señora Calveiro was watching her. "Believe it or not, but I am not looking for a husband."

"You have a lover in England?" he inquired in a low voice, and her cheeks flamed once again. He had no right to ask her such a question, and she was tempted to tell him so. But then it occurred to her that perhaps this was a means of defense, and straightening her spine she said levelly, "There is someone—yes," and had the satisfaction of knowing that for once she had disconcerted him.

Then, with a brief shrug of his shoulders, Luis got to his feet again. "I would say he is a foolish man, *señorita*," he remarked, winning the point after all. Pushing his hands into the pockets of his jacket, he gave her a polite nod before walking silently away.

To Caroline's relief, the party broke up soon after. In spite of her fears Don Esteban remained sober enough to wish farewell to his guests, and she made her escape in the melee, desiring only the peace and seclusion of her room. The shadowy corridor had never seemed longer, with the knowledge of Doña Isabel's presence behind one of the closed doors, but she reached her room without mishap and leaned back wearily against the panels.

What a tangled web her thoughts had created, darting and weaving among the jumbled threads of their relationships. If only Esteban's wife had still been alive; if only Luis had been her employer. And yet, did not the two things contradict themselves? If Luis had been her employer she would not have wished for him to have a wife. She hardly knew what she wished anymore. She was tired. It had been a long day. And even if she stayed only for the probationary month, there were still more than three weeks to go....

CHAPTER SIX

IN THE MORNING things looked different.

Caroline had slept shallowly, and she awakened early, spending several minutes on her balcony watching the sun's rays color the sky. It was another beautiful morning, the air cool and refreshing, the distant shimmer of the ocean like a mirage on the horizon. The heady scents from the garden below her windows filled her room, and although she knew that later the heat would make the flowers droop, now they blossomed voluptuously, spreading their velvety stamens and reaching greedily for the sun.

She rested her elbows on the balcony rail and cupped her chin in her hands. This was her fourth day at the hacienda, she thought pensively. Was she going to give it up so easily? Was she really going to admit defeat and return to her home in England?

She sighed, aware of her uncertainty now that the sun was shining again. Had she not perhaps overreacted to circumstances that were new to her? Was she oversensitive to other people's criticism? After all, she was not like them, and their restrictions should not be allowed to interfere with her determination. She was letting their attitudes influence her decision, and that had to be foolish.

Señora Calveiro was to blame. It was she as much as anyone who had put the doubt in her mind, intimating that Caroline might be interested in Don Esteban, insinuating a relationship that was wholly imaginary. No doubt she had her own daughter's future in mind, and it was true that Don Esteban might present an eligible image. A widower with only one child, not too old and undoubtedly wealthy. If Josetta appeared to prefer his brother to Don Esteban, that also was not important, for wasn't it already decided that Don Luis should follow his mother's example?

Caroline's teeth dug into her lower lip; she was unable to deny any longer the apprehension she felt when she thought of Luis's departure. It was ridiculous, she knew, but somehow she felt safer with him around. Yet that in itself was crazy. What had she possibly to be afraid of here? Don Esteban might drink too much, but he was a civilized human being, not some perverted monster who threatened her virginity. Emilia was just a child, and Doña Isabel, for all her eccentricities, was frail and elderly. She was more than a match for any of them, she told herself, and shutting all thoughts of Luis from her mind, she went to take her shower.

Half an hour later, in a white camisole top and black-and-white-patterned skirt, she left her room and walked quickly along the corridor and down the stairs. It was too early for the maid to bring her breakfast, and she had decided to take a walk outside before the heat became too oppressive.

She opened the door into the anteroom that she and Luis had used the previous morning, and then tried the door that led outside. It was locked. There was no key to turn to give her her freedom, and no matter how she tried, the heavy wood would not budge.

Frustration brought a beading of sweat to her forehead. *Damn*, she thought, *damn, damn, damn*. She knew the panicky feeling of a prisoner confronted by the irrevocable boundaries of his cell. Not that the hacienda bore any resemblance to a prison, she thought, struggling against hysteria, but its cloying atmosphere was suddenly stifling.

Turning away, she clutched at the handle of the door that bore the crucifix nailed to its surface. The iron latch lifted easily, and she drew back to allow the studded wood its outward passage, peering half apprehensively into the shadowy interior beyond the door.

A flight of stone steps led down, and licking her lips, she ventured forward. It was cool in the draft wafting up from below, and she wondered rather anxiously whether there were dungeons below the hacienda. Had the Spanish built dungeons below their palaces? She thought somehow they had, and while this was not a palace, it was very old.

But the light grew a little stronger as she reached the bottom of the steps, and what she had thought was another door turned out to be heavy velvet curtains concealing the chamber that now confronted her. It was a chapel, a small but exquisitely-decorated chapel, with a damask-covered altar illuminated by candles. The screen behind the altar was intricately carved and there were statues of the Virgin and Child, and another of the patron saint of San Luis de Merced. The statues were gowned in richly textured robes, glittering with precious stones, and the altar cloth and velvet kneeling hassocks were brilliant splashes of color within the chapel's gray walls. It was so vivid and so unexpected that she caught her breath, and the man who had been kneeling almost out of sight behind one of the stone pillars that supported the roof of the chapel turned to gaze half angrily at her.

It was Luis, unfamiliar in a long black cassock, his expression mirroring his impatience with her for having interrupted his devotions. Caroline's feet took her backward, seeking the soundless anonymity behind the curtains.

"Wait!"

His harsh admonition arrested her, and she faltered, watching his forceful approach with uncertain eyes. Seeing him like this was unnerving somehow, a confirmation of what hitherto had seemed scarcely credible, and her own emotions clawed inside her, making a mockery of the frozen face she turned toward him.

"I'm sorry," she said as he neared her. "I didn't know, I didn't think—" She broke off as he halted in

front of her, then added awkwardly, "The door into the
garden was locked. I couldn't find the key."

Luis studied her anxious face with a dark intensity,
then made an indifferent gesture. "It is no secret that I
come here," he said, gesturing at the altar. "It is the
only place in my father's house where I feel truly at
peace." She noticed he did not say his *brother's* house.
"But you wanted to go outside. I will show you the
way."

"Oh, please. . . ." Caroline put out a hand. "Do—do
go on with—with whatever you were doing. I mean,
don't let me disturb you. . . ."

Luis looked down at her imploring fingers and then
bent to haul the long black robe up and over his head.
Beneath he was wearing a black shirt and corded pants,
and he thrust the enveloping tunic aside and ran
smoothing fingers over his hair.

"Come," he said, starting through the curtains, and
with a curiously dry mouth she followed him up the
steps and into the anteroom.

The outer door was still immovable, and bidding her
wait for him, Luis disappeared into the main body of
the house. He returned a few moments later weighing a
handful of keys between his fingers. After a moment's
examination he found the one that opened the door.

"My brother becomes more security conscious as he
grows older," Luis remarked, turning the key. "This
door was never locked in my memory."

Caroline recalled what Doña Isabel had said about
the use of the *puerta accesoria*, and colored. Perhaps
Don Esteban had had the door locked to prevent the
woman his aunt had seen from entering the hacienda?
The woman they both believed was Luis's mistress!

"Is something wrong?" Luis had observed her sudden stillness, and Caroline forced herself to move past
him, out of the door and into the sun-drenched morning
air.

"Why—no. What could be wrong?" she responded
tautly, turning her face up to the sunlight, and then was

disconcerted still further when he fell into step beside her.

"Tell me," he paused. "Why do you think the door was locked? To keep you in?" He paused. "Or to keep someone else out?"

Caroline's tongue appeared briefly. "As—as you said, *señor*, your—your brother is aware of the value of his possessions...."

Luis snorted. "But you do not believe this?"

Caroline bent to touch the petals of a scarlet hibiscus, growing with others in wild profusion beside the zig-zag paving of the path. She was glad of the diversion to hide her expression from him, and choosing not to answer him, she inhaled the flower's delicate fragrance. "Do you know," she said, brushing pollen from her fingers, "people pay a lot of money for plants like these back in England. We have to keep them indoors and cultivate them carefully, whereas here they grow like weeds."

She heard his angry intake of breath, and the impatient oath that slipped unbidden from his lips, but she did not turn. He strode past her, leading the way down shallow terraced steps to a trellised rose garden. She hesitated for a moment, but then, shading her eyes against the glare, she followed him, treading the path that wound between sculpted banks of foliage. There were bees buzzing among the flowers, butterflies rose in startled flight as her shadow crossed their path, and the natural barriers of nature closed around them like the walls of a maze.

The path gave out beside a lily pond, where exotically colored fish darted among the trailing blossoms. Occasionally they came to the surface to feed from the suicidally reckless insects that skimmed the still water, and the rippling sound they made reminded Caroline that it must be almost time for breakfast. But when she turned, Luis was standing right behind her, blocking her path, and she was obliged to walk around the pond to put some space between them.

"I leave tomorrow morning," he said at last, when

Caroline, who had been searching her thoughts desperately for something to say, was almost at the end of her tether. His words fell like chips of ice between them. "This may be the last time we meet. Tonight I have to attend a wedding in the village, and tomorrow I shall be gone before you awake."

"I—I see." Caroline swallowed hard. "I—I—we shall miss you."

"We?"

"Emilia and I," she declared defensively, and he inclined his head in silent acquiescence. Then, "Will—will you be away long?"

"You mean, will I be coming back?" he amended harshly, pacing slowly around the circuit of the pool. "Not for some time, I think."

"Oh!"

Caroline was shocked at her own reactions to this. Even after what had happened this morning, even after seeing him in the robes of the priesthood, she could not reconcile herself to his calling. He was a man, and he disturbed her as no other man ever had, not even Andrew, she acknowledged unwillingly, and the emptiness his going evoked inside her was a physical thing.

"I—I'm sorry," she said now as he reached her, stopping to lift one booted foot and place it on the raised balustrade that surrounded the pool. "I—I know Emilia—"

She broke off abruptly, unable to go on beneath the level scrutiny of those dark-lashed gray eyes. She could not continue mouthing platitudes when she was so overwhelmingly conscious of the hard strength of his body only inches away from her own, and her complicity filled her with shame.

"Will you stay?" he asked now, turning his head to look at her.

She endeavored to present a calm facade: "Stay?" she echoed, her mind blank for a moment. "Oh—oh, you mean here...at San Luis. I—I honestly don't know." She moved her shoulders helplessly. "It... depends."

"On what?"

He was persistent, and expelling her breath unsteadily, she made a helpless gesture. "Whether—whether my—my work is satisfactory, whether your brother is happy with Emilia's progress, whether I—I find the work rewarding...."

"And that is all?"

She bent her head, the silky strands of pale hair falling around her ears. "I suppose you're referring to what I said last night," she ventured. "About...about Señora Calveiro."

"She had appeared to upset you. Or was that Esteban?"

Caroline shook her head. "I was tired last night. I may have been a little...hasty."

"So you will stay?"

"I don't know, do I?" She lifted her head, and her eyes, wide and indignant, met the naked passion in his.

"You must go," he said with sudden violence. "I do not want you here. Go home. Go back to England. Go back to this man who cares for you in a way I cannot understand."

Caroline's breathing quickened. "What do you mean?" she whispered, gazing at him tremulously. "What has my staying to do with you?"

Luis's mouth hardened. "I should say nothing, of course, should I not?" he retorted. "You are here at my brother's instigation. You are his employee. And if you were a little reckless in accepting a situation so far from the people and places you are used to, that also should not be my concern." He made a savage gesture. "But it is! It has been so ever since I saw you in the hotel in Las Estadas, and although I tell myself I should care nothing, that you are old enough to make your own decisions, you are a constant cause of vexation to me!"

"I'm sorry." Caroline was taken aback. She had not

realized he might feel concern for her. "I assure you I'm perfectly capable of taking care of myself."

"Are you? *Are you?*"

Without another word he put out his hand, his fingers curving behind her nape under the silky swath of her hair. Although she would have drawn back, his grip was purposeful, compelling her irrevocably toward him, drawing her against the upraised curve of his leg. Her hands, balled against his chest, were no defense against his strength and determination, and he bent his head without effort and covered her mouth with his.

His kiss was light and soon over, his lips barely brushing hers, and stiff, as if he held himself in check. "You see!" he said, and he was unable to conceal the raw emotion in his voice. "You are as helpless as a baby in the hands of a strong man, and you must realize my brother is no celibate!"

Caroline quivered in his grasp. "As you are."

"As I am," he conceded harshly.

Caroline moistened her lips. "A—aside from the woman—the woman who comes from the village," she choked impulsively.

The darkening anger of his expression was evidence enough of his comprehension. "So. You have learned a lot in a very short time, *señorita*," he grated, releasing her abruptly and removing his foot from the balustrade. "And already you are prepared to think the worst."

"I didn't say that." Caroline's legs felt like jelly but she had to go on. "Is—isn't it true? Is there no woman?"

Luis hunched his shoulders. "Oh, yes," he said, and his response caused a pain to twist like a knife in Caroline's stomach. "Oh, yes, there is a woman. Her name is Maria Pascale." His lips twisted as he turned to look contemptuously at her. "And what do you think we do together, when she comes here?"

Caroline moved her head helplessly from side to side. "It—it—it's nothing to do with me."

"You brought it up," he reminded her.

Caroline expelled her breath unevenly. "We'd better go back." She lifted her head. "Goodbye—*señor*. I—I hope you have a good journey."

Luis returned her gaze broodingly, making no move to leave. "You really believe it, do you not?" he demanded grimly. "You really accept that I could have a mistress!"

Caroline shook her head. "I've told you—"

"It is nothing to do with you, I know. But that is not good enough, *señorita*. I find I do not like to be humored like a recalcitrant child."

"*Señor*—"

"No. I will not be treated like this. I am a man, *verdad*! Do you not think that it is hard enough for me to try to forget, without your insinuating evidence of a relationship that is abhorrent to me!"

"I'm sorry." Caroline pressed her palms together anxiously, but he was not to be placated.

"Sorry?" he echoed, his eyes smoldering. "You are always sorry, are you not, *señorita*? Unfortunately, 'sorry' is not always good enough."

"Oh, Luis. . . ."

His name slipped carelessly from her lips, and although she caught her breath at its passing, it was clearly audible. She stood with lips parted, waiting for the censure she was sure was to come, and with the certain knowledge that her reckless tongue had destroyed any chance of a reconciliation. In any circumstances she had no right to think of him by his given name, and added to his earlier condemnation, it was a total indictment.

Shaking her head helplessly she turned away, taking deep gulping breaths of air, and as she did so she felt him move behind her.

"Luis," he said, and the way he said his name was so much more disturbing than the way she had said it. "You called me Luis," he added, his breath fanning the nape of her neck. "You should not have done that."

"I know, I know," cried Caroline tormentedly, bending her head over her twisted fingers. "Oh, why don't you just go away and leave me alone? All right, so I was insolent. Can't you just forget it? You're leaving soon. Does it really matter?''

"It matters to me," he responded in a low voice, and she started violently when his hands closed on her waist and impelled her back against him.

"What are you doing?" she exclaimed frantically, trying to push his hands away, but then she felt the powerful masculinity of his body molding itself to hers and her legs almost gave out on her.

"Caroline," he breathed, rubbing his tongue against the throbbing pulse behind her ear and her resistance dissolved.

"You... you shouldn't do this," she protested huskily, but her shoulders were yielding against his chest, her head tipping to one side to accommodate his probing lips. She could feel every hard muscle of his body, and for a few moments it was enough to know that he had forgiven her.

"I know what I should or should not do," he contradicted her huskily. "And I do not think my soul will be eternally damned for just holding you in my arms."

Caroline stiffened at his words, but he would not let her go, and her resistance melted again when his strong hands slid up over her rib cage to find the rounded fullness of her breasts, and the groan he uttered was one of anguished submission.

"This—I should not do," he muttered, twisting her around in his arms. "But I have to." And before she could make any protest, his mouth sought the trembling sweetness of hers.

Caroline's lips parted beneath the sensuous invasion of his touch, and her conscience was submerged in the urgent tide of emotion that swept through her at that moment. Luis's mouth was firm and insistent, his tongue hungry in its possession, promoting an intimacy between them that would not be denied. It was a breathtaking, suffocating submission of her identity, and her hands groped for him almost blindly. Almost without her volition her arms were around his neck, her fingers twining in his hair, her nails raking his scalp as she sought to hold him closer. She had never felt such a total devastation of her senses. Her whole body was flooded with a feverish excitement, and the intoxicating scents of the garden around them mingled with the musky male scent of his skin to sensitize her awareness.

It was Luis who eventually pulled away, leaving her with an empty, distraught feeling that threatened to overwhelm her. She felt sick and giddy, seduced by her emotions into a state of complete submission, and his withdrawal left her feeling weak and disoriented.

"So...what do I say now?" he muttered harshly, thrusting savage fingers through his hair. He looked grimly into her drugged features. "Do I apologize? Do I beg your forgiveness? Or is it too late to pretend I did not want to make love to you?"

Caroline moved her head bemusedly. "Don't say anything," she ventured faintly, struggling to regain her own composure, but the ugly expletive he used abused her attempt at understanding.

"No?" He spoke violently, and she realized how disgusted he was with himself for having allowed this to happen. "We just forget all about it, is that it?" His face twisted. "Of course. I forgot. You are an emancipated English girl. You are used to men making love to you. It means nothing to you!"

"That's not true!" Caroline was stung into retaliation. "I am not used to *men* making love to me!"

"Your lover, then. This man who cares so much about you he is prepared to allow you to travel halfway across the world without his protection!"

"Andrew is *married*!" declared Caroline tremulously, wanting to hurt him as he was deliberately hurting her. "That's why I'm here. That's why he didn't try to stop me!"

Luis's features froze. "You are in love with a married man?"

Caroline didn't know anymore, but she couldn't tell

him that. "What—what if I am?" she countered, and then knew a moment's agony when she saw the real torment in his face.

Shaking her head, she turned away from him and heard the sound of his footsteps retreating from her. She guessed her words had destroyed any lingering feeling he might have felt for her, and while that knowledge was painful, Luis might find some comfort in it.

CHAPTER SEVEN

THE DAY AFTER LUIS'S DEPARTURE, Don Esteban came
to the library while Caroline was giving Emilia her
lessons.

It was a day of rain, a steady driving downpour that
ran in rivulets across the windows and reduced visibility
beyond them to nil. It was much different from the rain
Caroline was used to, and when it had awakened her
that morning, pattering against the windowpane, she
had lain for several minutes considering how it reflected
her mood.

She supposed that after every bereavement there was
a period of time when one was too numb to really
understand the inevitability of what had happened, and
Luis's departure was like a bereavement. The knowledge that she might never see him again was too painful
to contemplate, and she was living in a state of bemused
insensibility.

She had not seen him again after that disastrous scene
by the lily pond. As he had predicted, he had been absent for dinner that evening, and the following day at
lunch Don Esteban had taken much pleasure and satisfaction in announcing his brother's departure.

"We will all miss him, will we not, *señorita*?" he
had remarked as they took the midday meal together as
usual on the terrace. If there had been any hidden meaning behind his suavely spoken words, Caroline had been
too distraught to notice it.

Yet, for all that, life went on, and although at times
the hopelessness of her feelings for Luis and the per-
manence of their separation were like a massive weight
bearing down upon her, she forced herself to behave as

she had always done, continually keeping all futile thoughts at bay.

The question of whether or not she would remain at San Luis after her probationary month was up was still far enough distant not to be of any immediate threat, but sooner or later it, too, would have to be faced. There were times when desperation drove her to think longingly of home, and others when the thought of leaving Mexico—and putting thousands of miles between her and Luis—filled her with despair. The likelihood that Don Esteban would find her work unsatisfactory was always a possibility, but at least with Emilia she found some measure of relief.

"Tío Vincente is gone," the little girl said the morning after Luis's departure, and burst into tears. Comforting the child, Caroline found comfort herself.

"Why do you call him Tío Vincente?" she asked after Emilia had dried her tears.

The little girl's chin quivered. "My mother used to call him Vincente," she said simply, picking up her pencil again. Caroline applied herself to the textbooks with a gladiatorial determination.

The advent of Don Esteban was an unexpected diversion. Apart from assuring himself of his daughter's application to work, he had shown little interest in her progress, and Emilia herself looked apprehensive when he stepped into the library. He had been absent at dinner the night before, and Caroline had nervously shared the meal with Doña Isabel. This morning, however, he was as immaculately dressed as usual, only the pouches beneath his eyes bearing witness to a possible overindulgence.

"Good morning, Miss Leyton. Good morning, Emilia," he greeted them silkily, closing the door behind him and advancing into the room. "But not such a good morning weatherwise, is it? Much more the sort of weather Miss Leyton is used to, I fear."

Caroline looked up from her books. "Can I help you, señor?" she inquired politely. "Would you like to see how Emilia's work is proceeding? Her English essays are really very good.''

''I am sure I shall have no complaints about your work with Emilia, *señorita*,'' her employer assured her smoothly. ''In all honesty, books and learning were always a source of boredom for me. I find the practical applications of experience far outweigh the knowledge acquired from books, and while it is important that Emilia should learn these things, they are not the whole meaning of existence, would you not agree?''

Caroline made a helpless gesture. ''If you say so, *señor*.''

''If I say so?'' he questioned, coming to stand beside the desk, the pungent fragrance of his after-shave lotion a sharp assault on her nostrils. ''My dear Miss Leyton, you must agree with me. Why else did you leave the familiarity—the security—of your home in England, if not to gain practical experience?''

Caroline put down her pen and linked her fingers together. She was aware of Emilia listening to their exchange with an intent expression upon her face, and although Don Esteban's words seemed innocent enough, she mistrusted his bland assertions.

''In what way can we help you, then, *señor*?'' she ventured, endeavoring to appear cool and relaxed. ''If you wish to speak with Emilia, I can easily prepare this lesson elsewhere.''

Don Esteban made a soothing movement, his plump fingers spreading over the desk. ''It is you with whom I wish to speak, *señorita*,'' he replied, moistening his thick lips. ''It is a privilege that I have denied myself, but that I am told has not been denied to others.''

A faint color invaded Caroline's cheeks. ''What did you want to say, *señor*?'' she asked stiffly. ''Naturally, as my employer, you have first call on my time.''

Don Esteban expelled his breath half impatiently. ''Do not be so—touchy, *señorita*. I was not criticizing you. I appreciate that while Luis was here your loyalties were divided.''

Caroline froze. "I don't know what you mean, *señor*."

"Of course you do," Don Esteban sighed. "It was perhaps unfortunate that I was...indisposed on the day of your arrival. Luis's deputation on my behalf enabled him to influence your thinking, and it was natural that you should regard him as your—how shall I put it—protector?"

"Don Esteban—"

"*Señorita*, I understand. My brother has always had this effect on women. They like him. They trust him. And he always lets them down."

Caroline drew an unsteady breath. Emilia's eyes were wide now and the curiosity in their depths was vaguely hostile. She was unlikely to understand what was going on, Caroline guessed, but any criticism of Luis was bound to create antagonism.

"I think this discussion could be concluded at another time, *señor*," she declared now, casting a meaningful glance in his daughter's direction. "Perhaps over dinner this evening." Emilia was always in bed before dinner. "But now, if you don't mind, we really should get on."

A brief shadow of impatience crossed Don Esteban's face at her words, but it was quickly dispersed. "Of course, of course," he averred placatingly. "But I think you misunderstand me, *señorita*. I did not come here to discuss my brother. On the contrary, Luis is of no further concern to any of us." He smiled, his lips curling back with a smugness she only faintly comprehended. "As it happens, I am driving into Las Estadas this morning, and I wondered if you and Emilia would care to accompany me. As it is such a miserable day I thought the outing might—divert us."

Caroline caught her breath. It was the last thing she had expected, and observing Emilia's astonishment, she guessed the suggestion had surprised the child too.

"As it is almost a week since you arrived at San Luis, *señorita*, I thought you might welcome the opportunity of visiting the shops or posting some letters," her employer continued affably. "We are so remote here, and it is fitting that you should have some free time."

"I have plenty of free time, *señor*," Caroline told him uneasily. "Emilia and I work only in the mornings, and the rest of the day is my own."

"But even schoolteachers must have a morning off sometimes," Don Esteban insisted. "So? Will you come?"

Caroline looked doubtfully at Emilia. Obviously the child would welcome the outing, and it was true that she had letters to mail: she had written to her parents the night before. But spending several hours in her employer's undiluted company was something else.

"Perhaps—perhaps Emilia would like to accompany you, *señor*," she faltered awkwardly. "I, er, I have these lessons to prepare—"

Don Esteban's expression hardened. "Is not my company to your liking, *señorita*?"

"Of course not. I mean—of course it is." Caroline flushed in embarrassment. "I just thought—"

"I shall be leaving in fifteen minutes, *señorita*. I suggest you wear waterproof clothing. As you are probably aware, the amenities at Las Estadas leave a lot to be desired!" And without giving her a further chance to protest, he strode arrogantly out of the room.

"You had better get ready, *señorita*," Emilia remarked after the door had closed behind him. "Don Esteban does not like being kept waiting."

Caroline, whose nerves were feeling decidedly strained, cast her pupil an irritated look. "Must you call him that?" she exclaimed, shuffling the textbooks together. "He is your father, Emilia. Whether you like it or not. And no amount of wishful thinking will make it otherwise."

"No, he's not." Emilia's chin jutted. "And don't you talk to me in that tone of voice. I know why you are upset—because Tío Vincente has gone away. But as Don Esteban says, Tío Vincente cares nothing for any woman since my mother died."

Caroline felt the first twinges of a headache probing at her forehead. "You imagine things, Emilia," she declared, striving desperately for a way to avoid spending the day in her employer's presence. "And perhaps you should go and change, too. That dress is scarcely suitable for tramping around Las Estadas."

Emilia shrugged. "I don't care."

Caroline sighed. "Don't you want to go?"

"With Don Esteban? No."

Caroline shook her head. "We don't have a choice, do we? Go and get ready. You heard what your father said."

Emilia gave her a mutinous look as she left the room, but Caroline was too distrait to notice. It was obvious that she would have to go, and after closing Emilia's exercise books she went to change her shoes.

She was hurrying back along the corridor when Doña Isabel's door opened, and her heart sank as the old lady emerged and spoke to her.

"You are going out, *señorita*? Is that not rather foolish on such a day?"

Relieved to find the old lady was lucid, Caroline forced a smile to her lips. "Emilia and I are going to Las Estadas with Don Esteban," she explained. "With luck it may have stopped raining by the time we get there."

Doña Isabel frowned. "You are going with Esteban?"

Caroline sighed, hoping this was not going to cause problems. "Yes."

Doña Isabel looked at her closely. "You like Esteban, *señorita*?" she queried. "I thought Luis said—but no matter. No doubt you know your own mind best."

Caroline pressed her lips together to stop them from trembling. "What did Don Luis say?" she asked, but already the old lady's mind was wandering.

"You take care, *señorita*," she warned, and the glitter of her dark eyes caused Caroline's pulse to quicken. "The Montejos are not to be trusted. As poor Vittoria found out."

Caroline shook her head. "Doña Isabel, Don Esteban's mother is dead—"

"Do you think I do not know that?" The old lady was suddenly very erect. "I know my mind wanders sometimes, but if I confuse Esteban with his father, that is because they are so alike."

Caroline nodded. It was easier to agree. "I must be going, *señora*," she murmured uncomfortably, and started when the old lady suddenly gripped her wrist with a bony claw.

"Esteban wants you, *señorita*," she hissed, her breath redolent with the sickly scent of parma violets. "Do not ask me how I know. I do. And if you think you will have any choice when the time comes, then you are a fool!"

Caroline tore herself away. "I think you're imagining things, *señora*," she declared, though the hand that massaged the reddened skin of her wrist was not quite steady. "I must repeat, I am Emilia's governess, that is all. Anything else is pure fantasy on your part."

All the same, as she left the old lady to walk quickly along the corridor, Caroline felt decidedly shaky. It was easy enough to tell herself that the old lady was eccentric, inclined toward the very fantasies she had accused Caroline of, but nevertheless it was unnerving to be constantly at the mercy of those unwarranted attacks.

Downstairs Don Esteban was waiting for her, dark and unfamiliar in an oilskin jacket. He looked with approval at her kneelength boots and dark blue mackintosh, and then urged her toward the heavy doors with a careless gesture of his hand.

"Emilia..." she said, glancing around anxiously, but there was no sign of her pupil, and her patience wavered. Where was the child? Surely she would not disobey her father. Remembering the last occasion that had happened, Caroline wished she had been more forceful.

"Emilia is not coming," Don Esteban informed her carelessly, swinging open the outer door and gazing at the drenching downpour. "*Dios mio*, will it never cease?" And without giving her chance to reply, he started down the flight of steps.

"Oh, but—*señor*—" Caroline hastened after him, pulling up her hood as she emerged from the porch. "*Señor*, what do you mean? Where is Emilia? Why isn't she coming with us? If she's not ready, then surely we can wait."

The Range Rover stood waiting at the foot of the steps, and Don Esteban gazed up at her impatiently. "Come, *señorita*," he called, and his expression brooked no argument. With a sigh of puzzled uncertainty, Caroline hurried down the steps.

"Emilia—" she said once more as he bundled her into the front of the Range Rover, and irritation marked the sensual fullness of his lips.

"Emilia is delicate," he declared, slamming the door and walking around the vehicle to climb in beside her. "It would not do for her to catch a chill, as she easily might, subjected to the weather. It is better that she remain at home."

Caroline gazed at him aghast. "Then isn't it better that I remain here, too?" she protested as he reached purposefully for the ignition switch. Don Esteban merely shrugged his heavy shoulders.

"Just because Emilia is a weakling is no reason why you should be denied the outing," he retorted, setting the vehicle into lurching motion, and she realized she had been deliberately tricked into accompanying him.

She stared blindly through the side windows as they drove out of the inner courtyard and then down the drive to the gates. Old Gomez emerged from the lodge to open the gates at Esteban's signal, but although he saluted his employer, there was no sign today of the smile he had reserved for Luis. But then, today was hardly a day for smiling, reflected Caroline tautly, unable to forget what Doña Isabel had said. And although she was not alarmed by Don Esteban's behavior, she was angry, and she saw no reason why he should think he could treat her in this way.

"You seem upset, *señorita*," he remarked now as they negotiated the twisting road that led down to the village. "I thought you would welcome the opportunity to see a little more of my country, in daylight this time, even if the circumstances are not as I could have wished."

Caroline turned to look at him. "They are not as I could have wished, either, *señor*," she declared, making no effort to disguise her annoyance. "I was employed to teach Emilia, not to indulge in sight-seeing outings to Las Estadas. You must know that had I suspected Emilia would not be accompanying us, I would have refused."

Don Esteban's expression did not alter. "I see. You would prefer to go back, perhaps?"

"I would prefer to go back," she agreed.

Don Esteban inclined his head. "Very well. When we reach the village I will turn the vehicle around, and we will go back for Emilia." He made a dismissing gesture. "And if she contracts a fever, then we must hope she has the strength to overcome it."

Caroline's lips clenched. "If Emilia is delicate, it would be madness to take her to Las Estadas on a day like this," she exclaimed.

"It is your decision, *señorita*," he intoned flatly, and Caroline gazed at him in helpless fascination.

"You'd do that? You'd take your daughter with us? You'd risk her health—"

"*Señorita*, my wife was like Emilia." His thick fingers swung the wheel to avoid a pothole in the road, and Caroline groped for the rim of the seat to save herself from falling against him. "Juana was susceptible to every germ and virus that came her way." He grimaced. "Myself, I blame her parents. They used to treat her like glass." He uttered a short mirthless laugh. "And like glass she shattered, without even giving me the son for which I married her. Oh, yes—" as Caroline turned a disbelieving face toward him "—that was why I married her, *señorita*. San Luis needed a son and heir, and my father contracted the marriage for me. Unfortunately, he had no idea that it was Luis who Juana really wanted when she cast those soulful eyes in this direction."

Caroline blinked. "You speak so dispassionately."

"Why not? Juana never cared for me, and Emilia is like her mother." He hesitated. "But perhaps if I treat her a little less tenderly she will survive her first pregnancy."

Caroline expelled her breath with incredulity. "*Señor*, I can't let you do that."

Don Esteban's heavy lids narrowed his eyes. "How will you stop me, *señorita*?" he asked.

She could tell he was attracted by the prospect, so her answer came swift and slightly breathless, "We will not turn back, *señor*. I will accompany you to Las Estadas."

It was an arduous journey, the road slippery and running with water, the landscape dark and dripping with rain. Even when the downpour lessened sufficiently to let her see something of her surroundings, the encroaching wall of vegetation was grim and unyielding, giving only onto solid outcrops of rock, starkly chiseled to make way for the road. They passed through areas of cultivated land where the rampant undergrowth gave way to banana and coffee plantations. Occasionally a cow or a donkey wandered haphazardly into the road, causing Esteban to swerve and swear violently as the Range Rover's tires spun uselessly centimeters above the surface. But mostly the journey was accomplished in silence, Caroline too absorbed with what she had learned to pay much attention to Esteban's uncertain humor.

Las Estadas was just as depressing as she remembered it, but this time Esteban parked the Range Rover off the main street and, adjusting his jacket, jumped down into the road.

"I will show you the way to the post office," he said, walking around the vehicle and swinging open her door. "Come. I will help you down." His eyes mocked her. "I regret there are no sidewalks here."

Caroline could have done without his assistance, but

rather than antagonize him she allowed him to help her down onto the spongy surface of the road. For a moment she was close to him, aware of the flesh-softened muscles of his chest, her lungs filled with the powerful scent of his after-shave. She glanced up and found him looking down at her, and recklessly she took a backward step.

Immediately her foot was plunged into the murky depths of a puddle that had formed at the roadside. She tried to disguise her gulp of annoyance, but Esteban saw the consternation on her face and, taking her arm again, drew her forward.

"Sometimes it is better to bear with the devil we know than to tempt the devil we do not," he remarked, his tongue circling his already moist lips. "*Señorita*, you and I must come to an understanding." His expression was enigmatic. "But for now, the post office is this way."

Caroline bore the intimate possession of his arm around her waist as they crossed the road, but once they were on the other side she determinedly freed herself. She would rather walk in the puddles than have his hands upon her, she thought, revolted by his proprietory attitude, and she was relieved when they reached the shabby building that housed the post office.

"I have to go to the bank," Esteban remarked then, glancing thoughtfully around them. "I suggest you attend to your business here while I am absent, and meet me in half an hour's time at the hotel."

Caroline's mouth went dry. "The hotel?" she echoed. "The hotel where I stayed the night before...."

Her voice trailed away, but Esteban didn't appear to notice. "Allende's posada, *sí*," he declared shortly. "We will have lunch there before returning to San Luis. It is not the most desirable hostelry, I know, but it is the best Las Estadas has to offer."

Caroline nodded, but her reaction was unmistakable. As if aware of her reticence, Esteban compressed his mouth. "You find my arrangements displeasing, Miss Leyton?" he inquired heavily. "Or is the company not to your taste? You would prefer that my brother was here in my place, perhaps?"

Caroline stifled her gasp of astonishment at his words and forced herself to meet his accusing stare. "If—if I have given you that impression, I'm sorry, *señor*."

"Are you?" Esteban was evidently unconvinced. "Do you dislike me, Miss Leyton?"

"No!" But her denial was almost too quick, too vehement. "I, er, I'm getting wet, *señor*," she protested faintly. "May I go and post my letter?"

Esteban thrust his hands into his coat pockets. "*Muy bien.*" His shoulders hunched. "Do as you say. We will meet at the hotel in twenty minutes."

"Twenty minutes, *señor*?"

"How long does it take to post a letter?" he countered caustically, and turning, strode away across the muddy street.

The hotel was just as seedy as she remembered, the group of Mexicans sitting on the veranda, tipping back their chairs as they drank their tequila and watched the world go by, just as dead eyed and indolent. Caroline crossed the slatted boards on hasty feet, reaching the comparative privacy of the reception hall with relief, and then drew back apprehensively when Señor Allende himself appeared from the bar.

"*¡Hola!* It is Señorita Leyton, is it not?" he exclaimed, squinting at her in the poor light that filtered through the grimy windows. "*Qué quiere usted? Una habitacion?*" He chuckled maliciously. "*No se si puedo ayudarte.*"

Caroline was about to explain that she didn't understand what he was saying, when her employer's voice interrupted them.

"Miss Leyton does not require a room, Allende," he stated coldly, coming into the hall behind Caroline and laying a possessive hand on her shoulder. "But had she done so, you would have been wise to accommodate her, my friend, unless you are wishing to relinquish the tenancy of this establishment forthwith.''

"¡*Señor!* Señor Montejo, how could you think such a thing?'' The fat little proprietor almost prostrated himself before Esteban. ''Señorita Leyton and me—we were having what you call a little joke, no?'' He cast imploring eyes in Caroline's direction. ''Is that not so, *señorita*? Old José, he likes a little fun. You know it is so.''

Caroline wondered how funny it would have been if she had been seeking accommodation, but her conscience would not permit her to be the unwilling instrument of his downfall.

''Señor Allende did—provide me with a room the last time I needed one,'' she offered, avoiding the little man's eyes, and Esteban drew a harsh breath.

''So he did. On my recommendation.'' His expression was unyielding. ''*No obstante*, he would do well to remember to whom he owes his loyalties.''

Caroline thought so, too, judging by the expression on Señor Allende's face. Evidently Esteban was his landlord, but it was more than just fear of eviction that put that consternation into his eyes. In a town like Las Estadas there could be no future for anyone who fell foul of the Montejos, and she almost pitied the little man as he fawned on them. But when, in the course of his conducting them into the tiny dining room of the hotel and seating them at the best table by the window, she accidently intercepted Señor Allende's gaze, she was shocked by the fleeting glimpse of hatred she saw there. It was quickly concealed behind a mask of groveling servility, but the memory of it remained with her, disturbing and unnerving.

CHAPTER EIGHT

ESTEBAN drank too much that evening.

Back at the hacienda, watching him filling and refilling his glass during dinner, calling for more wine, finishing the meal with a decanter of brandy, Caroline experienced the same kind of discomfort she had suffered on her first evening in his home. But now there was no Luis to counteract Esteban's indulgence.

Without his brother to taunt and attempt to humiliate, Esteban turned his attention to Doña Isabel, making fun of her pitilessly, mocking her style of dressing and deriding her husbandless state.

"My aunt is no doubt still a virgin, *señorita*," he drawled, raising his glass in Doña Isabel's direction. "That is so, is it not, Tía Isabel? My father's aberrations did not lead him to look in your direction, did they, *tía*? For all your girlish smiles and blushes!"

Caroline cringed, but Doña Isabel weathered the storm of her nephew's cruelty remarkably well. So well, in fact, that Caroline suspected this was not the first time she had been the target of his sarcasm.

"Like your father, you cannot see beyond a woman's thighs, Esteban," she retorted smoothly, helping herself to more cheese. "You think it is all-important for a woman to find a husband. And yet Señorita Leyton has proved that a woman can have a career other than marriage and motherhood."

"Señorita Leyton is not in question here," retorted Esteban broodingly, pouring more brandy. "Do you really think she is still—how shall I phrase it—*virgo intacta*? Alas, I fear you are sadly out of touch with life as well as with sex."

Caroline blushed furiously, but Doña Isabel, spearing cubes of cheese with her knife and popping them into her mouth, just went on. "If you consider virility so important, Esteban, then perhaps you should look to your own record," she remarked, nibbling a cracker thoughtfully. "For a man who considers himself so...macho—is that the right word—you have been singularly unlucky in your partnerships. Your first wife died without giving you any children at all, and poor Juana could produce only a puny girl child—"

"*¡Basta!* Be silent!" Esteban's face convulsed with anger. "What do you know of anything, you stupid old *bruja*! No one ever asked you to—" He used a phrase Caroline refused to acknowledge, and then hunched his shoulders over the table. "My marriage to Margarita was no marriage at all, and Juana was always a feeble-minded hypochrondiac! How could either of them be expected to give me sons when they couldn't even fire a man's passion?"

Doña Isabel shrugged, unmoved by his insults, but Caroline sank lower into her seat. She had not even known there had been a wife before the unfortunate Juana, and she wondered what had happened to her when her inability to conceive had proved absolute.

"Perhaps it is you, and not Luis, who should enter the priesthood," Doña Isabel suggested, and Caroline was astonished at her audacity. "After all, Señorita Leyton has no doubt heard the rumors that Emilia may not be your daughter, and if that is so, there is no proof that you can provide an heir for the hacienda."

Caroline thought he was going to hit his aunt then, but although anger brought the hot color to his cheeks and his eyes almost started from his head, discretion—or perhaps respect for the sharpness of her tongue, which was more than a match for his—stayed his hand.

"Go to bed, old woman!" he said, sinking back into his seat, his fingers closing once more around the decanter. "I will provide an heir for San Luis soon enough." His eyes flickered briefly over Caroline.

"I shall not need Luis's assistance when that time comes."

To CAROLINE'S RELIEF the clouds had disappeared by the morning, leaving a day that was hot and very humid. But anything was better than being confined within the walls of the hacienda, and she and Emilia spent the first half of the morning identifying plants and flowers in the garden. It was Emilia herself who did most of the instruction, teaching Caroline the names of the plants and explaining their cultivation, but the little girl seemed to enjoy demonstrating her knowledge and Caroline was glad to be out of the heavily cloistered atmosphere.

"Did you enjoy your visit to Las Estadas, *señorita*?" Emilia asked as they crouched beside the prickly tongues of a cactus.

Caroline gave her charge a thoughtful look. "You did not accompany us," she remarked, brushing a leaf from the skirt of Emilia's dress, and the little girl gave a nod of acquiescence. "I would not have left you had I known you would not be coming with us."

Emilia shrugged and rose to her feet. "You wanted to go, didn't you? You could have said no."

"I suppose so." Caroline straightened, remembering the choice Esteban had given her. "Well, I'm sorry you were left alone."

"Oh, I wasn't alone," retorted Emilia, beginning to walk back toward the house. "I went down to the stables to talk to Benito. He let me play with Cabrilla. She is the foal of Tío Vincente's mare, Aphrodite, the one he let you use the day he took you riding."

Caroline stared at her. "You know about that?"

"Of course." Emilia was haughty. "He told me. But I would have found out anyway. Benito would have told me."

Caroline sighed. "I'm not at all sure your father would approve of your spending time down at the stables. Particularly not when you are so prone to colds and chills."

Emilia's indignation was unmistakable. "You may be prone to colds and chills, *señorita*, but I am not," she retorted, very much on her dignity. "And my father would not disapprove of my spending time with Benito. He, too, used to like to visit the stables when he was a little boy, and later on he and my mother used to meet there."

Caroline sighed. "You're talking about—Don Luis, aren't you?"

"Tio Vincente, yes." Emilia pursed her lips. "I've told you. Don Luis is my father. Why do you think he plans to enter the seminary? Because the only woman he ever loved is dead!"

Caroline realized that at her age Emilia could only be repeating what she had heard and fantasized about.

"Where do you find such melodramatic nonsense, Emilia?" Caroline struggled to keep her tone light, even though the child's words were disturbingly plausible. "Don Luis's mother—your father's stepmother—she has entered the church. It is she, and not your mother, who dictates your uncle's conscience."

"That's not true." Emilia stared at her mutinously.

"It is true," retorted Caroline sharply, annoyed to find she was trembling. "You must stop imagining things, Emilia. The only person you convince is yourself."

To CAROLINE'S ASTONISHMENT, dinner that evening passed without incident. The pouches beneath Esteban's eyes looked a little heavier than usual, but his manner toward his aunt had reverted to the patient, sometimes cajoling tolerance he had previously shown. His attitude and conversation were completely different from the night before; Caroline thought it was almost as if he were two people masquerading in the same body. She had heard that alcohol could change a person's character, but she had never witnessed such a phenomenon until now.

Her own relief was mixed with uncertainty, compounding as it did her own doubts concerning her position at San Luis. While the previous evening she had been convinced that she should leave as soon as her probationary month was up, tonight her fears seemed groundless, the inevitable result of an overactive imagination. Her sympathy for Emilia and the confusing identity the child was creating for herself seemed far more important than fending off Esteban's advances, and although she found him looking at her sometimes with curiously speculative eyes, she suspected his interest had been stimulated by her association with his brother. She doubted he knew the whole truth of that relationship. Indeed she prayed he did not. And she hoped that now that Luis was gone, Esteban's interest in her might wane accordingly.

During the following days life at the hacienda assumed a pattern, and gradually Caroline began to relax. Her mornings were spent working with Emilia in either the library or the garden, depending on the weather. She rested during the long hot afternoons, renewing her interest in Pope and Steinbeck from the wide selection available to her on the library shelves. In the evenings she dined with Esteban and his aunt, discussing the food, the weather and the progress Emilia had made that day. Although occasionally she endeavored to introduce a more stimulating topic, her employer seemed quite content to treat her as he treated his aunt. It was frustrating, after years of being regarded as the intellectual equal of the men she associated with, and she began to realize that Doña Isabel was not as eccentric as she appeared. She had had a lifetime of combating this kind of male dominance, and while it could not be denied that she did occasionally suffer from delusions, perhaps that was the inevitable outcome of a suppressed personality.

The routine was again disrupted by Esteban.

As on that other occasion, he came into the library and interrupted a biology lesson Caroline was conducting with the help of a butterfly she had captured in the garden. The glossy-winged creature was safely imprisoned inside an air-filled plastic bag, and Caroline had every intention of letting it go again once Emilia had had time to examine its complex structure and absorb its various functions. She was in the process of explaining how important its wings were, not only as a means of flight but also as a means of protection, when Esteban came into the room, and for once Emilia turned to her father in eager exclamation.

"Miss Leyton has captured a butterfly," she exclaimed, although Caroline noticed she still forbore to address him personally. "Come and look! Isn't it pretty? Don't you think the colors are beautiful?"

Esteban took up the inflated bag and held it critically toward the light. The insect crawled across the base of the bag, confined within its cocoon of silence, and Esteban's lips curved with mocking satisfaction. "So. They are a pest," he observed. His thick fingers curved over the globe and the helpless creature was thrown into a panic-stricken beating of its wings.

"You're frightening it!" cried Emilia, getting up from her chair and reaching for the bag. But her father held it just out of her reach.

"I should have thought Miss Leyton might more profitably be teaching you about the birds and the bees," he remarked tormentingly.

The little girl gazed up at him without comprehension. "The birds and the bees?" she echoed, and Caroline knew she had to intervene.

"Did you want to join our lesson, *señor*?" she inquired, firmly taking the imprisoned butterfly out of his grasp and handing it back to Emilia. "You may find my methods of instruction boring, but you're welcome to listen."

"I am sure I should enjoy that," agreed Esteban smoothly, his dark eyes lingering on the dusky hollow between her breasts just visible above the low vee of her smock dress. Automatically her hand moved to conceal it. "But that is not why I am here, *señorita*." He smiled, observing her instinctive gesture. "It is a fine day, warm and only a little humid. Perhaps you and Emilia would enjoy a visit to the coast."

"To the coast, *señor*?"

Caroline absorbed this blankly while Emilia put down the plastic bag and turned to her father eagerly. "You really mean it?" she exclaimed. "You will really let us go to Mariposa?" She caught her breath. "Will you be coming with us?"

"Alas, no." Esteban's mouth twisted regretfully, but Caroline sensed his inner excitement. She had registered little after that word "Mariposa," and she guessed his announcement had been deliberate, and Emilia's response all he had intended. "You would like to see the ocean, would you not, Miss Leyton?" he asked. "It is not far. A matter of fifteen—perhaps twenty miles by road. Tomas will accompany you. Always providing you would like to accept this invitation."

Taking a deep breath, Caroline chose her words with care. "If Emilia would enjoy the outing, then naturally I accept. It was kind of you to think of it, *señor*."

Esteban smiled, but Caroline knew he was enjoying her consternation; she could see it, and she wished she was a little more adept at hiding her feelings. But the news that Luis was only ten or fifteen miles away, across the river estuary, had devastated her. If she had thought of their separation in terms of distance she had imagined hundreds of miles between them, and to discover that he was so near and yet so far was at once painful and incredible.

"You did not know Mariposa was so near, *señorita*?" Esteban probed, and she knew he knew she did not.

"I knew the ocean was not far away," she responded quickly. "I can see it from my bedroom windows. I remember remarking on it to your brother."

"And he did not tell you how far away it was?" Esteban mocked.

"Oh, yes. He told me," she answered, and it was nothing short of the truth.

"But not that that was where the seminary was," Esteban persisted, and Caroline had to shake her head. "*¿No es verdad?* But you can also see the bell tower from your window, *señorita*. A reassuring sight, I am sure."

Caroline was equally sure it was not, and she wondered what had happened to bring about this sudden reversal in his character. Since the night after their visit to Las Estadas he had given her no cause for complaint, and if occasionally she suspected he was deliberately playing a role to disarm her, this morning he had certainly abandoned that part.

"So you will be ready to leave in a few minutes," he said. "I will have Tomas fetch the car to the door."

"Thank you."

Caroline looked at Emilia's expectant face and knew she could not disappoint the child, but as she went upstairs to freshen her makeup she wished she better understood her employer's motives.

It was impossible not to take the time to go to her window and look out across the stretch of land to the distant ocean. There was the sea glistening invitingly on the horizon, and beside it the dark shape of the bell tower, which previously had had no significance for her.

MARIPOSA was as different from Las Estadas as it was possible to be, unless perhaps the fact that the sun was shining made white-daubed houses look quaint instead of shabby. The town was approached by a tree-lined highway, and the main street faced the ocean. A narrow promenade circled the tiny harbor where fishing boats bobbed on their moorings, and the houses on the streets that ran up from the seafront had pinkish red roofs and flowers in the window boxes. A tiny market near the harbor offered fish and all kinds of fruit and vegetables, huge juicy melons jostling beside mackerel and whitebait, red snappers and yellowtails.

They had driven to Mariposa not in the Range Rover, as Caroline had expected, but in an elderly Bugatti that

Tomas treated with much reverence. He parked the vehicle by the harbor and then turned in his seat to address his passengers.

He spoke in Spanish and Emilia, realizing Caroline could not understand, translated. "He says he has some shopping to do for Consuella," she explained, after listening carefully to his instructions. "He suggests we...might like to go for a walk while he attends to his business."

"To go for a walk?" echoed Caroline thoughtfully, glancing at the curious faces all around them. "A walk...where?"

Tomas was beginning to look anxious. He began speaking again, more quickly now, gesticulating to Emilia and spreading wide his hands. Caroline wished she could understand even half of what he was saying, and she waited impatiently for the child's explanation.

"It's all right," said Emilia carelessly, lounging back in her seat. "He's only concerned that we should not get lost. But I told him I know my way around Mariposa. I shan't get lost."

Caroline sighed, and Tomas, gazing at her appealingly, started to speak again. She thought she caught the word *playa*, which she recognized as meaning beach, but apart from that his rapid chatter meant nothing to her.

"Are you sure he wants us to go for a walk, Emilia?" she asked, biting her lower lip, and Emilia's jaw jutted.

"I don't tell lies, *señorita*," the child retorted coldly, and Caroline made a placating gesture as Tomas climbed out of the Bugatti.

Emilia waited until Tomas had been absorbed by the crowds of people thronging the little marketplace before she pushed the front seat forward and, opening the passenger side door, climbed down from the vehicle. "Are you coming, *señorita*?" she inquired from the roadway, pulling the straw boater she was wearing firmly down upon her head. With a helpless movement of her shoulders, Caroline complied.

The sun was hot, but after two weeks Caroline was getting used to its brilliance, and looping the strap of her handbag over her shoulder, she followed Emilia along the salt-pitted promenade. They attracted some curious glances, but they were not accosted, and after a few moments Caroline began to look curiously around her.

She wondered where the seminary was situated and guessed it was probably on a rise, which would account for her being able to see the bell tower from her window. She looked up then and immediately saw the gray stone walls of a two-story building standing on a promontory overlooking the small town.

Her throat went dry as she gazed up at the unmistakable cupola of a bell tower, and then Emilia intercepted her stare and gave a knowing snort.

"That's not where Tío Vincente stays," she declared scornfully as Caroline tore her eyes away. "That's the Convent of the Sisters of the Annunciation, *señorita*. Where Tío Vincente's mother lives."

Caroline moistened her parched lips. "Then where—"

"Farther on. Across the river," answered Emilia offhandedly. "If you like, I'll show you where."

"Oh, I—" Caroline shook her head helplessly. "I don't think that's a very good idea, Emilia."

"Why not? You want to see where he stays, don't you?" The little girl's mouth was drawn down at the corners. "Don Esteban thinks so."

Caroline drew an uneven breath. "What possible interest could there be for anyone in seeing the gray walls of some religious academy?"

"I don't know," Emilia shrugged, her face sulky. "But you asked."

Caroline sighed. "I was curious, that's all."

Emilia looked at her broodingly. "Didn't you really know where Mariposa was?" she persisted. "I wonder why Tío Vincente didn't tell you."

Caroline endeavored to appear indifferent. "I suppose it has nothing to do with me," she replied, stopping to lean on the harbor wall, peering down into the gray-flecked waters that surged against the rocks. "We should have brought a shrimping net, Emilia. There are dozens of tiny fish down here, swimming around in shoals."

Emilia leaned on the wall beside her, but her interest was elsewhere. "Perhaps he doesn't want to see you, *señorita*," she remarked doggedly.

Caroline lifted her head to stare at her. "How could he see me?" she argued, wishing Emilia would leave it alone.

She caught her breath when the child replied casually, "He isn't a prisoner, you know. He sometimes comes into town. Don Esteban knew that when he sent us here. That's why he wanted us to come."

Caroline had just about had enough. Straightening away from the wall, she faced the child without patience. "I think you're imagining things again, Emilia," she declared tautly. "I've warned you before about the consequences of making up these stories." She pressed on determinedly, in spite of the little girl's whitening face. "You've been too long without playmates, people of your own age to mix with. You've become obsessed with things that any normal child would never think of." She paused and then finished raggedly, "You don't need a governess, Emilia. Personal relationships are beyond your comprehension. You should go to school, to a boarding establishment, where you won't have time to worry about your mother or your father, or find ridiculously twisted reasons for a perfectly innocent outing!"

It was a brutal setdown, and Caroline felt an immediate sense of contrition for taking out her own insecurity on the child. As soon as she had finished speaking she wanted to retract her words, but Emilia did not give her a chance to do so.

Her dark eyes wide and wounded in her white face, the child turned abruptly away from her governess, and

before Caroline guessed her intention, she had darted
across the road. Holding her hat on her head with one
hand, the other swinging in urgent motivation, she ran
rapidly up a side street disappearing swiftly among the
lines of drying wash.

It happened so quickly that Caroline was nonplussed.
By the time she had gathered her wits and hurried across
the road after the little girl, Emilia was nowhere to be
seen, and only vacantly staring faces confronted her
mute-lipped agitation. If only she knew the language,
she flayed herself impotently, and then hastened on up
the street, hoping that Emilia would change her mind
and come back

Whereas the sun had been only pleasantly hot on their
shoulders as they walked beside the harbor, now its rays
became a pitiless weapon, beating down on her merci-
lessly, soaking her limbs with sweat. The simple cotton
chemise she was wearing began to cling where it touched
her, molding her skin and outlining every curve of her
body. She soon tired in the unrelenting heat, and as her
footsteps slowed, the glare seemed to envelop and
devour her.

"¿Señorita?"

She heard the voice as if from a distance, the waves of
light around her seeming to bring its resonance on
receding swells of sound, her nostrils filled with the
pungent odor of dust and heat and unwashed humanity.
She blinked, but all she could see was the sun striking
off whitewashed walls. She was in another of the narrow streets that opened off each other like tunnels in a
rabbit warren, and her heart raced in panic as she realized how far she had come from the harbor.

"¡Señorita!" The summons was repeated.

Shading her eyes, she swung around, her legs pro-
testing as she poised herself for flight. She doubted she
could outrun anybody in her weakened state, but she
would try, even if she collasped in the attempt.

But to her astonishment she found only an elderly
man behind her, dressed all in black. Upon his head he

wore a curious round-brimmed hat, the crown shallow, that scarcely concealed his wispy threads of hair.

"*¿Puedo ayudar usted, señorita? ¿Se ha perdido?*"

Caroline didn't know what he had said, but his manner was gentle, conciliatory, and she expelled the breath she hardly knew she had been holding. "I'm afraid I don't speak any Spanish," she ventured without much encouragement, but the old man nodded as if he understood.

"*Inglesa,*" he said, and she understood that. "*¡Se ha perdido!*"

"I am looking for a little girl," said Caroline wearily. "*Una niña, señor.*" She put out her hand to indicate Emilia's size. "She ran away."

"*¡Una niña, señora! ¿Su hija?*"

Caroline blinked. *Hija*? That was "daughter," wasn't it? The man was asking if the girl was her daughter, and rather than confuse things still further, she nodded.

"A little girl," she repeated. "Emilia. Emilia de Montejo!"

"Hah, Montejo?" he echoed, obviously recognizing that name. "Emilia de Montejo? *¡Venga!*"

His bony fingers gripped her forearm while he indicated that she should go with him, and Caroline glanced around her helplessly. The women standing in the doorway of a house opposite were unlikely to help her if she cried for their assistance, but in any case she doubted the old man could prevent her if she really tried to free herself. She was torn between the awareness that she was lost and that he might conceivably be trying to help her, and the inevitable possibility that his frailty was just a shield for other men of more dubious appearance. She couldn't forget what Luis had told her about the ever present threat of a kidnapping, and the idea that Emilia might at this moment be in the hands of such men was terrifying.

Yet the old man had seemed to respect the Montejo name, and he looked harmless enough. What else could she do, after all? Return to the harbor without her charge? And no means of communicating with Tomas to gain his assistance!

Shaking her head, she let the old man draw her farther into the maze of streets, stumbling as a stone twisted her ankle and dodging the billowing lines of washing. She was so hot and weary she hardly noticed what way they were going, and while common sense told her she should keep alert, a numbing lethargy was addling her brain.

When they rounded a corner she felt a sudden draft of air on her face. Her astonishment was total, and she gazed in amazement at the mud flats of the estuary. Somehow, she didn't know how, they had emerged onto the coast road and ahead of them lay a narrow bridge over the river.

Her lips parted to make some futile protest, to explain that she would have to go back to find Emilia, when she saw two figures crossing the bridge. One was small and dark, dressed in white, with what looked like a straw boater on her head, while the other was tall and dark, unmistakably attired in robes similar to those of Caroline's companion.

And suddenly Caroline understood. The man who had rescued her was not some devious villain, but a priest from the seminary across the river. He had recognized the name because he knew Luis.

Her eyes darted back to the figures on the bridge, and as they did so, her heart plunged. It was Luis who was holding Emilia's hand, Luis who was returning her charge to her; and the old priest beside her folded his hands in satisfaction.

"*¡Allí está su hija, señora!*"

Caroline could have tried to explain then that she was not Emilia's mother, but she was too shocked to do anything but stand and watch Luis and the child as they came off the bridge and along the dusty road toward them. She felt sick with reaction, and weak with relief; but overriding everything else was the painful resuscitation of emotion, and the knowledge that separation from Luis would be harder a second time.

The old man greeted Luis warmly, offering his explanations in his own language. He used his hands a lot in the process, gesturing back toward the streets they had negotiated, pointing at Emilia and rocking his head expressively from side to side.

Luis's response was curt and concise, the glance he cast in Caroline's direction eloquent of his disapproval. No doubt he blamed her for the whole sorry affair, thought Caroline wearily, pushing shaking fingers through the damp weight of her hair.

Emilia clung to Luis's hand, avoiding Caroline's eyes, her features still mutinous. Caroline wondered what Luis had thought when the child appeared at the seminary, and acknowledged that in his position she would probably feel angry, too. After all, the little girl must have run a fair distance. Looking across the estuary, Caroline could see the walls of a square building and guessed that was the seminary. But then, she thought, fanning her hot face with a languid hand, Emilia had known where she was going, while she had not.

Eventually the old priest ran out of things to say, and with a sign of benediction he bid them *adiós*, trudging off up the road again toward the bridge. Caroline managed to thank him before he went, but he only shook his head in deprecation, wagging his finger at Emilia as if admonishing her for her recklessness.

Alone with Luis and his niece, Caroline felt completely exhausted and totally incapable of handling the argument that she was sure was to come. The excitement of seeing Luis again had dissipated in the cold shadow of his disapproval, and although her heart ached in anticipation of his anger, she felt too weary to defend herself.

"Father Enriques tells me you were lost when he found you," Luis remarked at at, looking at her intently. "*Dios gracias*, he did! You appear to be on the verge of collapse. How did it happen? How did you and Emilia get separated?''

Caroline opened her mouth to protest, but then saw Emilia's anxious expression. Obviously the child had not told her uncle the whole truth and was waiting with tight-lipped hostility for Caroline to explain what had happened.

But Caroline felt too fatigued to comply. What did it matter, anyway, she thought dully. Emilia had been lost, but now she was found. Let that be an end to the matter.

"Emilia and I were walking together," she said now, slowly. "There were a lot of people around. We got separated. I had to look for her."

Luis's grays eyes narrowed, the long silky lashes shadowing his expression. That he didn't believe her was evident in the glitter in their depths and the skeptical line of his mouth, but Caroline told herself she didn't care. He was so cold, so remote, so detached from her world in his long black gown tied with a plaited cord. A gold cross hung from his belt, glinting in the sunlight, reminding her with painful intensity that whatever had been between them was irrevocably over. She told herself she didn't care what he thought of her; she meant nothing to him. But her treacherous senses craved his forgiveness and yearned for a contact he could not give.

"Where is Tomas?" he demanded now, and Emilia, recovering from her relief at being exonerated of all blame, jerked back her head.

"He parked the car near the market," she said, permitting a tentative smile in Caroline's direction. "Miss—Miss Leyton and I didn't want to stay in the car, so we just went for a walk. Like she said," she finished lamely.

Luis's lips twisted. "Indeed." His eyes flickered over Caroline once again, and she became aware of how disheveled she must look. "Then I suggest we walk back to the harbor this way—" he indicated the coast road

"—and assure him that you have not disappeared off the face of the earth."

Emilia nodded eagerly, and Caroline reluctantly straightened herself from her lounging position against the seawall. She didn't honestly know if she had the strength to walk back to the harbor, but somehow she would have to do it.

Luis released Emilia's hand and the little girl ran a short way ahead of them, stopping every now and then to allow them to catch up. Luis walked with Caroline, the movement of his robes causing a faint draft against her bare legs. He seemed taller, more alien than she remembered, but just as disturbing to her emotional condition.

"You realize I do not believe you," he remarked in an undertone, his voice low and disruptive. "You and Emilia could not simply have become separated. And what is more, Tomas had instructions not to let you out of the car."

Caroline gasped. "How do you know that?"

Luis shook his head impatiently. "It is always so when Emilia leaves the hacienda. Unless Tomas or one of us is with her."

"I was with her," pointed out Caroline tautly, but Luis dismissed her presence with a wave of his hand.

"You are no bodyguard, *señorita*." He made a sound of contempt. "You cannot even take care of yourself."

Caroline glanced up at him resentfully. "Anyone can get lost."

"Especially in a strange town, where they do not understand the language." His fists clenched. "Do you know what could have happened to you if Enriques had not happened along?"

Caroline knew, but she would not admit it. "I can take care of myself, *señor*!" she asserted firmly. "Just because—"

"Just because—nothing!" he snapped. "You were— are—exhausted! You would have stood no chance at all if some man had taken it into his head to accost you."

He raised his eyes heavenward. "At least accept the truth for what it is. *Dios mio*, I died a thousand deaths when Emilia arrived at the seminary and told me she had lost you."

"Emilia did not lose me!" retorted Caroline sharply, then averted her eyes from his accusing stare. "In any case, I can't believe you were so concerned about me."

"Can you not?" His fingers tortured the knot of his belt. "Not even when I tell you I left the seminary without permission?"

Caroline's lips parted. "Oh, Luis! Luis, I'm sorry. But don't be angry with me, please. I don't think I can stand it."

She heard his sudden intake of breath and the shuddering exhalation that followed it. But when he spoke his voice was low and tormented. "Why did you come to Mariposa?" he demanded. "Why did you have to torture me like this? Have you any idea how hard it is for me, living here, knowing you are in Esteban's house?"

Caroline turned her head to stare disbelievingly at him. "But—your faith—"

"Oh, yes, my faith," he echoed harshly. "That is all-important, is it not? Unfortunately I do not have such faith in my brother!"

Caroline sighed. "Esteban told me where you were. He—he suggested this outing."

"He would," affirmed Luis grimly. "It pleases him to manipulate people. I just wish to God that you were anywhere else than at the hacienda. I do not trust him."

Caroline frowned. Then, assuring herself that Emilia was out of earshot, she said, "What do you mean? Why don't you trust him?"

"You," said Luis flatly, causing a prickle of apprehension to feather along her spine. "I do not trust his reasons for bringing you here."

"Me?" Caroline shook her head. "But Señora Garcia employed me—"

"Did she?" Luis sounded unconvinced. "I wonder."

"What do you mean?"

"Caroline—" he spoke her name huskily, and her legs felt suddenly weak. "—Esteban has been looking for a so-called governess for Emilia for almost a year. The interviews you attended were not the first. There have been many more, in both England and the United States."

"But—" Caroline was confused. "I thought—"

"Señora Garcia may have interviewed you, but ultimately Esteban had to make the decision." He frowned. "Tell me, was there anything unusual about your interview? Did you have to supply any photographs or anything?"

"No." Caroline tried to think. "At least, not proper photographs. Señora Garcia did say I ought to get a strip of photographs taken for a visa, but later on—"

"You didn't need them?"

"No."

"So what happened to them?"

"I don't know. Señora Garcia kept them, I suppose." Luis nodded. "They were sent to Esteban."

"How do you know?"

"They had to be." He expelled his breath heavily. "It was no accident that you turned out to be so...attractive."

Caroline made a helpless gesture. "But why should it matter to him what I looked like?"

"I think you know the answer to that."

Caroline trembled. "That's ridiculous!"

"Is it?" Luis gazed broodingly out to sea. "I wish I could be so sure."

Caroline touched his sleeve and then drew her fingers away as if it burned her. His moody eyes were turned on her. "Luis, why don't you come back to San Luis? Why can't you find another vocation? Esteban could employ you on the estate, I know he could. Luis...please—"

"I cannot," he said tautly, and her spirits plummeted. "You do not understand, and I do not have time to explain it to you."

"Find the time," implored Caroline urgently as they neared the noisy market square and she glimpsed Tomas standing by the Bugatti. "Luis, talk to me. Talk to me, please. You must. You must!"

"I cannot," he repeated harshly, and her shoulders sagged as Emilia came to possess herself of her uncle's hand once more.

"You will not let Tomas be angry with us, will you, Tío Vincente?" she begged, and her uncle looked down at her resignedly.

"Why should Tomas be angry with you, *pequeña*?" he inquired dryly. "Unless you disobeyed his instructions. Did you do that, Emilia. Did you lead Miss Leyton into danger?"

Emilia hunched her shoulders. "Miss Leyton heard what Tomas said," she said sulkily, but Luis would not allow that.

"Miss Leyton does not understand our language, Emilia," he reminded her severely. Then he allowed her to clamber inelegantly into the vehicle while he spoke to the chauffeur in his own language.

Tomas was so relieved to see them that he could only gabble effusively, shaking Luis's hand and evidently thanking him for restoring his two charges to him. Then Luis turned to Caroline.

"So," he said, and his voice was unusually thick as he made his formal farewell. "Look after yourself, *señorita*. And you, too, Emilia. I expect you to take care of Miss Leyton on these occasions. And if you promise to do so, I will forgive you."

Emilia's pale face lost its dejected expression, and bouncing forward on the seat, she leaned out to wrap her arms around Luis's neck. *"Te amo,"* she whispered, hugging him close. Over Emilia's shoulder Caroline saw Luis repeat the child's words.

"Tomas has agreed that he will say nothing of this to Don Esteban," Luis added as he put Emilia firmly back into her seat. "It will serve no useful purpose, and I think Emilia has had enough excitement for one day."

Caroline nodded, too numb at the prospect of his imminent departure to care one way or the other. With a stiff nod he stepped back. *"¡Vaya con Dios!"*

Caroline bent her head as the Bugatti pulled away, but Emilia turned and waved until her uncle was out of sight. Then she slithered around in her seat and looked half curiously at her governess.

"Didn't you like seeing Tío Vincente again?" she demanded. "I told you I knew where he was."

"Yes." Caroline was finding it hard to say anything. "But you shouldn't have run away."

"Well...." Emilia shrugged indifferently. "You were so horrible to me. I wanted to give you a fright."

"Which you did," confirmed Caroline tremulously. "Anyway—" she smoothed the skirt of her dress "—I suggest we forget all about it now. So far as your father is concerned, we had a pleasant outing and we didn't meet anyone."

Emilia bent her head. "Tío Vincente really likes you, doesn't he?" she persisted, causing Caroline's nails to dig into her palms. "He was really upset when I told him I didn't know where you were."

"Emilia, stop it!" Caroline's nerves were almost at screaming pitch. "Let's drop the subject. I never want to see your uncle again."

Emilia's speculative gaze said she didn't believe her, and Caroline couldn't altogether blame the child. She knew she must look as sick as she felt. But she could not allow Esteban to suspect that anything was wrong, especially after what Luis had told her. It would be easier if she went home, she thought, crushing the sense of despair that filled her at this admission. To go on hoping was just a foolish whim, and the longer Luis was at Mariposa, the more remote her dreams became. Better to go, to make a clean break when her month was up, to sever forever any chance of meeting him again.

She refused to consider the possibility that Esteban might not let her go. How could he stop her, she asked herself reasonably. She was a free woman, a British citizen; any coercion on his part would not be tolerated.

And yet when she arrived back at the hacienda the first place she looked was the library. Leaving Emilia to regale her father and Doña Isabel with the details of their outing, she entered the booklined room in search of the butterfly she had left imprisoned.

She did not have to look far. Someone, she had no way of proving who, had pierced a hole in the plastic bag, allowing all the air to escape. The butterfly was dead, its wings spread in its final battle for survival.

CHAPTER NINE

IT WAS FOOLISH to let the death of a butterfly upset her, but it did, and she could hardly bring herself to go downstairs again to face her employer. She had fled to her room after finding the pathetic corpse still lying in its plastic shroud, and even after washing her face and brushing her hair she was still in a state of shock.

She knew that seeing Luis had been the real agony, but nothing could alter the fact that she had been responsible for the butterfly's cruel demise. It was the manner of its death that troubled her most. If someone had crushed the insect, or trampled it to death, she might have understood. But to cold-bloodedly rob a living creature of air, so that every panic-stricken beat of its wings decreased its chances of survival, was the essence of a very subtle kind of cruelty.

Of course, she acknowledged, viewing her pale face in the mirror without satisfaction, she could be wrong. Esteban might have had nothing to do with it. There might conceivably have been a hole in the bag before they left. But none of these possibilities convinced her, and she went down to lunch feeling sick and uneasy and just a little frightened.

But as if the morning had never been, Esteban was the soul of consideration and politeness. Assisting Caroline into her chair at the glass-topped table laid on the terrace overlooking the pool with the stone jaguar, he set an iced fruit juice in front of her and then proceeded to discuss her outing with a geniality that quite disarmed her.

"Emilia tells me you did not have time to go to the beach, *señorita*," he remarked, helping himself from the tray of canapés placed beside him. Caroline acknowledged the conspiratorial look the little girl cast in her direction. "But you did see the market at Mariposa, and the harbor, so perhaps you can go to the beach another day."

"Perhaps," agreed Caroline noncommittally, sipping the freshly squeezed orange juice. "But I really think Emilia learns more from lessons than outings, *señor*. And I'm sure you want her to achieve the best qualifications possible."

Esteban smiled, his thick lips greasy from the meat oozing from the rolled banana leaf he had just put into his mouth. "I am sure we are all satisfied with your progress, *señorita*," he responded, licking his fingers. "I have never known my daughter to enjoy her lessons so much."

"You're very kind." Caroline forced a faint smile, but the conversation was not going at all the way she had intended. "However," she added carefully, "it has to be said that Emilia might benefit more from a more formal education, *señor*."

Fortunately Emilia had gone to feed the fish and was not listening to their conversation, but Doña Isabel had heard her words, and now she said, "You see, Esteban? Señorita Leyton's ideas are radical. I said as much before, if you remember."

Esteban shook his head, ignoring the old lady. "Emilia will not be going to the university as you did, *señorita*," he told Caroline pleasantly. "Therefore there is no need for a more...formal education."

Caroline took a deep breath. "Nevertheless I wonder if you realize how lonely your daughter is, *señor*. I mean...she has no playmates, no one of her own age to associate with at all. Don't you think she might benefit from the friendship of children her own age?"

Esteban raised his wineglass to his lips, studied her across its rim for a moment and then set it down again. "But this is amusing, *señorita*," he exclaimed, and gave a short laugh as if to prove it. "Anyone would think you wanted to be dismissed." He moved his shoulders expressively. "*Señorita*, I am quite satisfied with Emilia's education, and if you are so worried about her...isolation from children of her own age, then I am prepared to make a further concession."

"You are?" Caroline spoke faintly.

"But of course." Esteban frowned. "The Calveiros—you remember the Calveiros? Their eldest daughter is married and lives only a few miles from Las Estadas. She has two children nearing Emilia's age, a boy and a girl. I suggest I invite them to share lessons with Emilia, if you have no objections, and afterward there will be time for play before they have to go home."

Caroline felt weak. "I—I have no objections, *señor*. If—if that's what you want...."

"It is what I want, *señorita*," Esteban assured her firmly, and for the moment there was nothing more Caroline could say.

He was as good as his word. The following week Victor and Juanita Alvarez joined Caroline's morning classes, and in the effort required to bring them up to Emilia's standard, Caroline had little time to, worry about her own difficulties.

Victor was older than Emilia, but at ten he did not have her grasp of languages. Juanita was the same age but was quite backward in both writing and reading, and Caroline spent hours teaching her how to do the simplest kind of arithmetic.

Still, she acknowledged, it was good for Emilia. Because of her advanced abilities she was able to help Caroline with Juanita, and her own superiority increased her confidence a hundredfold. She and Victor almost came to blows half a dozen times during that first week, but gradually they all settled down.

It was revealed that their mother had been teaching them up to this point, but that in six months' time Victor was to attend the convent school in Mérida. Juanita would join him there when she was older. Caroline wished Esteban would let Emilia go there, too, but he seemed determined to keep Emilia at home, and she shrank from broaching the subject of her departure.

There were no more outings to Mariposa, but one evening Esteban suggested Caroline might like to join him for a ride the following morning. "Not on horseback, you understand," he said as she was struggling to find some reason to refuse. "I do not like horses. But in an open carriage I use to drive around the estate."

"But... the children—" began Caroline doubtfully. "Their lessons—"

"We will be back before it is time for lessons," retorted Esteban shortly, and she decided it would be easier to give in.

The next morning, however, she regretted her submission. The idea of sharing with Esteban something she had previously shared only with Luis filled her with reluctance, and the lowering skies above them seemed to emphasize her inhibitions.

The trap, for it was little more, awaited them at the stables, with the mare Caroline had ridden tethered between the shafts. Old Benito gave Caroline a dubious look as she climbed into the carriage beside her employer, but he refrained from commenting, aside from a muffled grunt in answer to Esteban's greeting. It was obvious that he, like Gomez, saved his affection for Luis, and she couldn't help wondering why their father had not divided the estate between his sons. It seemed so unfair that one should have all and the other nothing, but perhaps the law of primogeniture prevailed.

In spite of her apprehensions it was good to be outdoors again, though she still viewed the cattle with some unease. Riding in the carriage was not like being on horseback, and although she had been scared while riding, too, she had known she could outrun them if she had to.

However, Esteban showed no such misgivings. On the contrary, he drove through the herd without hesitation and stopped to speak to the drovers before driving on.

His destination was a knoll overlooking the swirling waters of the river, and after securing the reins he suggested they get down and walk for a while. "The ground may be spongy, but you're wearing boots," he observed when she hung back. With a fatalistic feeling Caroline accepted his hand.

He did not release her fingers, however, after she was safely on the turf beside him, and after a moment's futile effort Caroline had to voice her objection. "Please—let me go, *señor*," she begged him stiffly, and when he still did not do so she added, "Really, I am quite capable of walking by myself."

"I am sure you are, *señorita*," he remarked, raising her resisting fingers to his lips. "But I enjoy helping you, and I shouldn't like you to run away."

"There's no likelihood of that here, is there?" Caroline exclaimed, annoyed at the sudden tremor in her voice. "Please, *señor*, you're upsetting me. Have—have the goodness to release my hand."

"Very well." Esteban obediently let her go, and she immediately pushed her hands into the pockets of the short leather jacket she had put on over dark green corded pants. She was hardly surprised to find her palms were moist, or that the back of her neck felt damp, but her relief was so great she could dismiss these other symptoms of her apprehension.

They walked a short way, Caroline a few steps behind her employer, and then Esteban stopped again and turned to her. There was the lick of rain in the air, a heaviness evident in the ominous-looking clouds on the horizon, and she thought for a moment that he was going to suggest they turn back. But instead of this he faced her squarely across her path, and as she faltered he said, "I suppose you are aware that in a few days your probationary month with us will be up?"

Caroline expelled her breath unsteadily, aware that she had been expecting something more than this. But his question demanded an answer, and she strove to give it composedly.

"I—I am aware of it, *señor*," she said, endeavoring to hide her stammer. "It—it's been on my mind, as a matter of fact. The decision I have to make."

"The decision?" Esteban regarded her intently. "What decision do *you* have to make, *señorita*? Surely the decision is mine."

Caroline cleared her throat. "Well, yes. Yes, it is. But it's mine, too, *señor*. The—the probationary period is on both sides."

Esteban's dark brows descended. "You are not serious, *señorita*."

"Oh, but I am." Caroline licked her lips. "It—it was a big decision for me to make, *señor*, coming out here, leaving my home and my family. I—I had to try it, to see if I was happy here. There was no other way."

"And?" Esteban waited grimly for her answer.

"And...well...." Caroline was finding it increasingly difficult to go on. An image of Emilia's small face was imprinted on her mind, appealing to her, reproaching her, and although she told herself that if she were not there Esteban would have to consider the convent school, she dreaded the retribution he might take on the child.

"And what if I do not accept your decision?" Esteban suggested suddenly, interrupting her troubled thoughts.

"You—you want me to leave, *señor*?" Caroline held herself tensely.

"No." His response was what she had been afraid of. "No, I do not wish you to leave...Caroline." His use of her name made the hairs on the back of her neck prickle now. "I want you to stay. For always."

Caroline's lungs felt constricted, and she gazed at him disbelievingly. "I—I beg your pardon?"

"You heard what I said, *querida*." He took a step toward her, which she quickly nullified by taking a step backward. "I want you to remain at San Luis. Not just as Emilia's governess—but as my wife!"

"You—you don't mean that!"

Caroline turned it back on him in an effort to gain some time, but Esteban was adamant.

"I do mean it. I mean every word of it." His knuckles traced the paling hollow of her cheek. "Do not look so alarmed. It is quite a compliment I am paying you."

Caroline shook her head, flinching from his touch as if it repelled her. Which it did, just as he did. Like a snake! She fought for reason, trying to think coherently through the haze of disbelief and blind panic that fogged her brain. But all she could think of was her helplessness and her vulnerability, and the isolation of her situation here at the hacienda.

"What is the matter, *querida*?" Esteban was not blind, and her reaction to his proposal was all too evident. "Surely Luis warned you of my determination to have a son. I cannot believe that during those...intimate conversations you had with him, he did not confess his hope that one day San Luis de Merced might be his!"

"No!" Caroline was appalled. "No, he has never—"

"But you did realize that if I could not provide an heir, the estate would revert to my brother?"

"I never thought about it." Caroline made a helpless gesture. "It has nothing to do with me."

"Oh, but it does." Esteban stepped toward her again, and this time his hands on her shoulders prevented her from backing away from him. "Caroline, do not look so anxious. I am not threatening you. And naturally, I realize, you need time to think it over." He drew her inexorably toward him, his dark eyes hypnotic in their intensity. "But do not take too long. I am not a patient man, and you must understand, I am eager to tell the world of my good fortune."

His words brought her to her senses. With a determined jerk she was free and facing him bravely. "I can't," she said, and there was a desperate note in her voice. "I can't marry you, *señor!*. I don't love you, and although I realize that isn't a necessary part of marriage in your country, it generally is in mine." She took a deep breath. "I, er, naturally I'm flattered." She swallowed the lie with some effort. "But I'm afraid I have to refuse."

Esteban made no immediate response, and as they stood there facing each other the rain began to come down. It fell heavily, huge globules of water that could soak a man in seconds, pattering noisily on the seats in the carriage, whispering in the grass at their feet. It quickly soaked Esteban's dark hair, running in rivulets down his forehead and into his eyes. He cursed irritably, raked back his hair with a careless hand and then glanced angrily around at the carriage.

"We'd better go back," murmured Caroline cautiously, half-relieved by the advent of the storm. At least it had cut short Esteban's protests, she thought; and leaving him, she started tentatively across the grass toward the carriage.

Esteban overtook her before she had taken half a dozen steps, passing her aggressively, climbing into the two-wheeled vehicle and releasing the mare's reins. The little carriage lurched forward as the first clap of thunder reverberated ominously across the plain, and Caroline started to run as she realized what he was about to do.

"Wait!" she exclaimed, stumbling as she ran, wiping the blinding torrent out of her eyes. But Esteban ignored her. With reckless abandon he whipped up the mare, setting her at a gallop, leaving Caroline to gaze after him with a sickening sense of disbelief.

The carriage soon disappeared into the mist that shrouded the plain and hid the hacienda from her sight. Even the herd of cattle was invisible, somewhere between her and safety. She was at least two miles from her destination, rapidly getting soaked to the skin, with the certain knowledge that Esteban would send no search party out to look for her.

Panic threatened to overwhelm her. It would be so easy to give in to the tears that were pricking the backs of her eyes, and succumb to a sense of despair. But she knew that if she allowed herself to give up, if she stayed where she was and waited until someone came to find her, she could well die of pneumonia or exposure or both, and although she felt desperate, she was also furiously angry.

Feeding this anger, realizing it was the only thing likely to keep her going, she set off across the plain in the direction from which she thought they had come. The ground, already spongy before the downpour, was a quagmire, but although her legs ached with every step she took, she persevered.

It was the smell of the cattle that alerted her to their proximity, and her nerve almost gave out when a group of the beast loomed up in front of her. She realized how helpless she was, without even a mount to save herself on, and wondered if she had any chance of coming through them unscathed. What if she missed her way? What if she trudged around in circles, unable to find her way back until the rain stopped? It was frightening how unfamiliar things could seem when there was no landmark to cling to.

The thunder rumbled again, accompanied by a searing flash of lightning, and the cattle stirred in protest. Caroline was terrified. She knew storms had been known to stampede a herd, and her own position among the animals was hopelessly precarious. But this was the way Esteban had come. She knew of no other way. And did she really have any choice?

Ignoring her fears, she pressed on, avoiding the brooding brown eyes raised to watch her passage, praying that the cattle would pay her no heed. It seemed hours since she had left the knoll beside the river, and the rain just kept on coming down and down. Her pants were soaked, her boots squelched with water, and the shoulders of her jacket were heavy with moisture. Her hair was plastered to her head, and although she was sure it was dripping down her neck, the uncomfortable wetness was all one with the drenching cascade of the storm.

The ferocity of another flash of lightning caused her to make a little sound of alarm, and the cattle nearest to her shifted restlessly. Caroline clapped her hand over her mouth, silencing any further sound she might make, and stumbled on tearfully, her legs weak and unsteady. She was not going to make it, a small voice inside her taunted, and in all honesty she was beginning to wonder if she could.

The low murmur of voices when it came to her seemed like an extension of her own inner protest. It came to her ears through the steady tumult of the rain, mingling with the movements of the cattle, the lowing sounds they made as they shifted from one grazing spot to another.

She halted uncertainly, half-afraid she was having hallucinations, but there was definitely someone within calling distance. The trouble was, she was afraid to call for fear of alarming the cattle. Straining her ears, she endeavored to move in the direction from which the voices had come.

The sound receded, and devastation gripped her. Was she going in the wrong direction? Had she somehow missed her way in her haste to make contact with another human being? Were sounds distorted by water, deflected by so many solid objects?

She realized she was moving with more confidence through the cattle, actually forgetting her fear of them as she strove to reach her goal. She no longer started every time a horned head was turned in her direction, and she told herself with determination that she was going to make it.

When the flash of lightning illuminated the bivouac beneath the trees, she could hardly believe it. Someone had stretched a waterproof sheet between two branches. She stood beneath its improvised shelter, shaking with reaction.

She was alone, but the evidence of recent occupation was all around her. A metal coffeepot simmered on the ashes of a fire, and there was the smell of fresh meat and cornbread. Obviously the drovers had been having breakfast, and the voices she had heard had come from here.

Bending she groped for a metal cup, and ignoring the dregs in the bottom, she poured hot coffee into it. Then, still crouched, she raised the cup to her lips, shivering as the steaming liquid ran warmly into her stomach.

"¡Hola! ¿Qué quiere usted?"

The harsh male voice that accosted her brought her head up with a start, and she got unsteadily to her feet. The rainwater had darkened her ash-fair hair, but as the man looked at her her identity was unmistakable, and his mustachioed lips parted in an expression of ludicrous disbelief.

"Señorita!" he exclaimed, and then, as another man followed him into the shelter, he turned to speak to him in a garbled patois.

Caroline could not understand what they were saying, but she was so relieved to have found shelter that she hardly cared. Her limbs ached and she was soaked to the skin. Sooner or later she would have to come to terms with Esteban's abandonment of her, but right now she could only be grateful for another human's company.

The men turned to her then and spoke in slow careful Spanish. "¿Qué hay? ¿A dónde va usted? ¿Dónde está Don Esteban?"

Caroline faced them wearily. She guessed, after recognizing Esteban's name, that they were asking where he was. Perhaps they thought she had abandoned him, she mused half hysterically, then forced herself to speak calmly as she tried to make them understand.

"Don Esteban, er, a hacienda," she murmured helplessly. "You take me there?"

She gestured as she spoke, pointing to herself, then out into the rain—toward her destination, she hoped.

The men looked troubled. Obviously they were concerned that Don Esteban was not with her. Maybe they imagined she had thrown him into the river, she thought, feeling weak at the thought of having to go and look for him.

They held a whispered conference, arguing together, glancing frequently in her direction, evidently deciding whether to believe her. Caroline waited heavily, the weariness of reaction coming over her, and she gazed at them bleakly when they eventually touched her arm.

"Venga, señorita," one of them said encouragingly, gesticulating toward where their horses were tethered. And with a sense of inevitability Caroline followed the men outside.

The rain was lessening slightly, although the thunder still rumbled in the distance. The storm was abating, and with it came the tremulous awareness of having to face her employer with her resignation.

She was given a mount, a spirited palomino that was more accustomed to rounding up stray cattle than to being bridled. Caroline clung tightly to the reins, unable to decide in what direction they were going, and wondered rather headily what she would do if the men proved unreliable. If they had recognized her, however, it was unlikely that anything unpleasant would befall her, she consoled herself. Her own experiences of Don Esteban had proved that he was not a man one crossed lightly.

When the horses began the ascent to the gates of the hacienda, she could hardly believe it. She was safe, she thought joyfully, and then revised that opinion. She was back at the hacienda, that was all. She still had to stomach whatever manner of retribution Esteban might devise for her refusal.

Gomez opened the gates and gazed at her in astonishment. The words he exchanged with the man accompanying her apparently gave him no satisfaction, either, and Caroline's head ached from trying to piece together what was being said. Something about Esteban, she hazarded, feeling totally exhausted, and she could hardly swing her legs across the saddle when they reached the shallow flight of steps.

The door was opened almost as soon as she had dismounted, and as on the occasion of her arrival at San Luis, Consuella appeared at the head of the steps.

Her shocked exclamation was intelligible in any language, and she hurried down the steps urgently, uncaring of the persistent drizzle. She caught Caroline around her waist as her legs buckled beneath her, and half carried her into the house with the aid of one of the maids she summoned.

What happened next was just a blur to the exhausted girl. She was aware of hands supporting her as she climbed the stairs to her room, of other hands stripping away her clothes and of the painful protest of chilled limbs suddenly thrust into warm water. No one mentioned Esteban, and she wondered if he knew she was back. But not until she was wrapped in warm towels did Doña Isabel appear to ask questions.

"You are feeling better?" she inquired, waving away the girl who had been toweling Caroline's head with an imperious hand. "The servants tell me you came back alone, that Esteban was not with you. Would you like to tell me where he is?"

Caroline gasped. "He's not back?"

"That is what I said." Doña Isabel arched her thin brows. "What happened? Was there an accident? Has Esteban been hurt?"

The dispassionate tone of this inquiry chilled Caroline's blood, and yet, remembering how Esteban had tormented his aunt, she could hardly blame the old lady. "I don't know where he is," she exclaimed, plucking anxiously at the soft bath sheet. "He—he—we got separated. I assumed he had come back here."

"But now you know he did not," retorted Doña Isabel sharply. "What took place between you? I presume there was some...contretemps?"

Caroline felt a hysterical desire to laugh. "You could put it like that," she admitted huskily. "He—he asked me to marry him, *señora*."

Doña Isabel showed no surprise. But then, why should she, thought Caroline wearily. She had suspected this all along. Instead she folded her gnarled hands tightly together and walked stiffly across to the windows.

"You did not accept." It was a statement, and Caroline conceded the point. "He was angry."

Caroline sighed. "He drove away and—and left me."

Doña Isabel made a sound of impatience. "*¡Idiota!*" she mouthed grimly. "You could have been trampled to death!"

Caroline bent her head. "You don't think—"

"No." Doña Isabel turned to her. "Esteban has more sense than that." But she frowned all the same. "*No obstante*, his absence is a cause for concern, and I have instructed a search party to investigate immediately."

Caroline acknowledged this silently.

"So, *señorita*?" The old lady was very much in control. "You will be leaving San Luis?"

Caroline nodded.

"It is for the best," Doña Isabel agreed. "Esteban would be better to turn his attentions toward Señorita Calveiro. She, at least, would know what to expect."

It was lunchtime before Esteban was found and brought back to the hacienda. Apparently the carriage had overturned in the mud, and like Caroline, he had been forced to walk back. Unfortunately, it appeared he had walked in the wrong direction, and remembering how angry he had been, Caroline was not truly surprised. However, he was soaked to the skin, as she had been, and chilled by the length of his ordeal. She watched through a crack in the library door as he was helped up the stairs.

Emilia, ever inquisitive, discovered from Consuella that the doctor had been sent for, and Caroline was relieved when Esteban did not appear for either lunch or dinner. She herself was still very much shaken by what had happened, and it was enough to have to answer Emilia's questions.

She dreaded having to tell the child that she was leaving. Although they were not close, a certain rapport had sprung up between them. Given time, she felt sure they would have become firm friends. But that was impossible now, she had to accept it, and she waited apprehensively for the moment when Esteban would learn of her decision.

CHAPTER TEN

.THE FOLLOWING MORNING Caroline awakened with a sore throat and a snuffly nose. She guessed her soaking the previous day had made her susceptible to the virus, and she was unutterably relieved to discover that the storm had made the roads so bad that Victor and Juanita would not be attending lessons. Emilia was sorry not to see her playmates but sympathetic to Caroline's condition, and the morning passed without incident within the quiet walls of the library.

At lunchtime Caroline steeled herself to face her employer, only to find her efforts had been futile. Esteban was still indisposed, and Doña Isabel seemed curiously unwilling to discuss his condition.

"He will send for you when he wishes to see you, *señorita*," she declared, spearing a sweet potato on her fork. Caroline could only feel relief at this second, unexpected reprieve.

"Why did you not come back with him?" Emilia asked again as she and Caroline were leaving the morning room. "I thought you had been out alone, but Consuella said you went out together."

Caroline sighed. "We—we had an argument, and I decided to—to walk back." She crossed her fingers. "Then it started to rain."

Emilia accepted this without comment, but Caroline could see she was not completely satisfied. However, the child did not pursue the subject, and Caroline delivered her into the hands of a nursemaid before making her own way to her bedroom.

Esteban did not appear at dinner, either, and there was a curiously expectant atmosphere about the household that Caroline had not noticed before. Maybe they were more concerned about their master's health than she knew, she mused thoughtfully, but they had never previously given her that impression.

She went to bed early, her cold symptoms combining to give her a throbbing headache, and she slept almost immediately, drugged by the aspirin she had taken with some water.

She awakened to a darkened room and blinked for a moment, wondering what, or who, had aroused her. Switching on the lamp beside her bed, she examined the hands of her watch. It was just a little after one o'clock, and she had slept for only three or four hours. She doubted she would have woken without any reason. At least, not for another three or four hours.

Sliding out of bed, she pushed her feet into soft mules and groped for the satin wrapper that matched her nightdress. It was useless to pretend she was not now completely alert, and she decided she would read for a while before attempting to sleep again.

But first she opened the door into the corridor and peered out tentatively, listening for any sound. The lights in the corridor were still on, which was unusual, she thought. Leaving her bedroom door ajar, she tiptoed along to Doña Isabel's room. Perhaps the old lady was sick, she thought. Perhaps she had cried out. Whatever her opinion of Doña Isabel, she would not like to think of her lying there helpless when she was only a few feet away.

She put her ear against the panels, straining to hear any irregular note in the old lady's breathing, and then almost fell over when the door was suddenly opened and she was catapulted into the room.

Recovering herself with as much dignity as she could muster, she opened her mouth to apologize to the old lady sitting up in the square four-poster. But then she realized it was not Doña Isabel who had opened the door, and her eyes darted swiftly to the tall man standing to one side of her.

"Luis!" she breathed, half-convinced she really was hallucinating this time. His dark face convulsed in a spasm of emotion. But before he could say anything, Doña Isabel interposed, her appearance curiously vulnerable without the elaborate coiffeur she usually effected.

"What do you think you are doing, *señorita*?" she demanded severely, pointing an imperious finger. "How dare you stand listening at my door! You told me you had a headache, that you were going to take some medication and have an early night. How long have you been eavesdropping on our conversation?"

"I didn't. I mean—I haven't." Caroline glanced helplessly at Luis, appealing for his assistance, but he seemed like a stranger to her. "Doña Isabel, someone—something—woke me up. I—I thought you might be ill. . . ."

"And you came to find out?" suggested the old lady skeptically.

"Yes." Caroline sighed. "I'm sorry if I'm intruding." Her hand went nervously to the neckline of her robe. "I—I apologize. If—if you'll excuse me. . . ."

She turned back into the corridor, intent only on putting herself out of their sight. But, as if suddenly galvanized, Luis came after her then, excusing himself from his aunt with a gesture and closing the heavy door behind him. "Wait!" he said. "*Señorita*, wait!" And then, more heavily, "Caroline. . . do not shut your door against me. I must talk to you."

Caroline halted in the doorway to her room. "Well?" she said tremulously, viewing his dark-robed figure without approval. "You don't have to worry, you know. I did not eavesdrop on your conversation. I really did think your aunt might have called out, or I wouldn't have left my room."

Luis sighed, supporting himself with one hand against the wall beside the door, massaging the back of his neck with the other. "I have not said I disbelieve you, have I?" he argued, meeting her indignant gaze. "The door to my aunt's room slammed in the draft. That is probably what disturbed you. I offer an explanation."

Caroline nodded. "Very well. You've solved the problem. Now you can go back to your aunt and continue your secret discussions—"

"They are not secret discussions," Luis interrupted her impatiently, but Caroline would not have that.

"What would you call them, then?" she demanded. "You come here at the dead of night, obviously so that I—so that *no one*—knows you're here—"

"You do not understand."

"No, I don't. And I don't want to. If you'll let me close my door—"

"Caroline, stop this!" His expression had hardened into a taut mask. "You have no right to behave as if I had committed some crime! I am here at my aunt's invitation—"

"I don't want to know why you're here," she retorted, too hurt and confused to care what she said. "Go back to your seminary. I'm leaving anyway. In a few days I'll be back home in England, among people who live simple, ordinary lives—"

"And with this man who already has one wife?" inquired Luis grimly, and the small spurt of resistance went out of her. With her lips pressed tightly together she turned away, shaking her head as she did so. After a swift confirmation that the corridor behind him was empty, Luis stepped into the room after her and closed the door.

Caroline turned as the door thudded into place, and caught her breath in disbelief when she saw Luis standing in front of it. "What do you think you are doing?" she exclaimed, half-troubled by his strained expression. He rested back against the panels, probing his temples with finger and thumb.

"We have to talk," he got out harshly, closing his eyes for a moment as though the knowledge pained him. "There are things you must understand before you judge me so uncharitably."

Caroline drew a deep breath, feeling the need to justify herself. "I—I am not judging you," she said. "I just don't want to be involved!"

"Is that true?"

He looked at her then, the gray eyes bleak with some dark emotion, and her lids fell before his. "You know... it's nothing to do with me," she said, choosing her words with care. "This—this family is not my concern...."

"And hasn't my brother made it so?" demanded Luis roughly, straightening away from the door so that he towered over her like some avenging spirit. "Is it not true that Esteban has asked you to be his wife?"

Caroline looked up. "Well, yes. But I refused—"

"And you think that will be the end of it? Your refusal?" He sneered. "You are so innocent in some ways, señorita!"

Caroline stiffened her spine. "I don't know what you mean."

"I think you do." Luis drew an impatient breath. "Oh, Caroline, I know my brother. He is sick at present, but when he gets better—"

"I shall be gone," said Caroline with trembling dignity. "Are you trying to frighten me, señor? Because, I should tell you, I do not scare so easily."

Luis sighed, shaking his head. "As when you walked home through the cattle?" he suggested. "That was brave, sí. But human beings are not as predictable as cattle."

Caroline sought the bedpost, clinging to it with both hands. "What are you trying to tell me, señor? What do you want to say? It's late and...and I am tired. And I know you did not come here to see me!"

"You do not know anything," responded Luis tightly. "However, you are right; this is not the time or the place to go into such things. Why I am here is of more immediate importance at this time."

"Why you are here?" Caroline's fingers massaged the carved wood in her grasp. "But why you are here has nothing to do with me."

"You are wrong," he retorted grimly. "It has much to do with you. Unfortunately, that is why it must be kept...confidential."

Caroline was more confused than ever. "Why?"

Luis expelled his breath heavily. "Tía Isabel sent for me. My brother is ill—"

"You mean...he's dying?" Caroline was appalled, but Luis quickly shook his head.

"No," he said flatly, fingering the crucifix at his belt. "I was not brought here to administer absolution. He has merely developed a fever as the result of exposure. With bed rest he should recover completely."

"Then, what—"

"It is the state of his mind that concerns Tía Isabel," declared Luis quietly. "He has been—how do you say it—making certain wild statements concerning your relationship."

"Our relationship?" Caroline's lips parted. "I don't understand."

Luis moistened his lips. "He seems to be of the opinion that you...will change your mind."

"No!"

"But yes. And Tía Isabel thought I should be informed." His twisted smile was wry. "Not because she has any liking for you, *señorita*, it must be said, but because she does not wish the name of Montejo to suffer the blight of another scandal."

"An—another scandal?"

Luis bent his head. "You told me Esteban had explained our relationship."

"Well, yes." Caroline licked her lips. "You mean—"

Luis sighed. "Esteban's mother, Vittoria, killed herself. She was the victim of our father's intrinsic indifference to anyone's interests but his own." He paused. "My mother suffered some guilt, I know, but she was as helpless to resist his charm and attentions as anyone else." He shrugged. "He was that kind of man. He inspired affection in both men and women alike."

As you do, thought Caroline urgently, but she said nothing.

"So, you see, Tía Isabel is concerned about what may happen when Esteban is well again. She thinks that you should leave as soon as possible. And I endorse that view."

Caroline's lips quivered. Of course. He would, she thought bitterly. As long as she was here at San Luis, she was both a threat and a temptation.

"I see," she said now, looking down at the soft folds of apple-green satin that clothed her body so closely. "So what have you decided?"

"You will leave tomorrow," said Luis expressionlessly. "Tomas will drive you to Las Estadas, and from there you can pick up the bus to Mérida." He shook his head. "The arrangements are not entirely to my satisfaction, I will admit; but it is the way you came, and it is the best I can offer. Tomas will see you safely aboard the interstate transport, and once in Mérida you should have no difficulty in booking a flight to London."

"Thank you."

Caroline had tried to speak composedly, but the words were husky, and Luis noticed.

"You will be happier in England, as you say," he intoned heavily. "With your own family and . . . friends." He paused. "Tell me, this man you had an affair with . . . you will meet him again?"

His voice had harshened, and Caroline glanced at him a little apprehensively, suddenly aware of the lateness of the hour and their isolation in this quiet room.

"Andrew?" she ventured carefully. "Well, yes. I may see him. He—he and his wife live quite near us. He—he's a lecturer at the same university as—as my father."

Luis's face was a graven mask. "And he is the kind of man you most admire?" he continued in the same tormented tone. "A man of culture and sophistication, who treats you as his intellectual equal and can sustain your interest?"

Caroline swallowed rather convulsively. "He—he is an intelligent man, yes," she admitted. Then, "Luis, why are you asking me this? What does it matter to you how I intend to live my life? You don't want me—"

"Do not be a fool!" With a muttered curse Luis stretched out a hand and in a swift sure movement grasped her arm to draw her closely against him. Through the rough wool of his gown and the thin transparency of hers, the hard muscles of his body bit into her, the male scent of his skin invading her nasal passages. Her face was scraped by the coarse fibers of his robe. Though her lips were parted she was suffocatingly deprived of air, her hands curling against him impotently yet clutching the cloth where it came within her reach. "Of a surety, I want you," he grated, his mouth against the silky softness of her hair. "And not even my mother, and the humiliations heaped upon her, can prevent me from admitting that I am as weak as my father was—"

Caroline's murmur of protest was stifled against his lips, breathed into his mouth and melted by the heat of his passion. No gentleness this, but the eager hungry urgency that demanded complete surrender. One hand was gripping her nape, holding her still for his possession, the other loosening the cord of her negligee, sliding beneath the wrapper over the smooth sensuous down of the satin. Her nightgown was low at the back, and his fingers, finding the deep vee, caressed the sensitive curve of her spine. She arched against him involuntarily, opening her mouth beneath his searching tongue, and a mindless sweetness invaded her senses. She had hardly known what it was to want a man, to feel the need that tore away inside her like a living thing fighting for survival. She wanted to feel him close to her, without the restricting confines of their clothes. Almost blindly she pressed herself against him, eager for whatever he cared to do with her.

"¡Por Dios, Luis!"

The choked exclamation came from Doña Isabel,

who, having thrust open the door, now stood in the aperture. A brocade robe concealed her nightgown, and her dark hair hung in two stubby plaits on either side of her appalled face. That Luis turned at once from Caroline in no way seemed to appease her. Her wild eyes glittered with a malevolent fire, and Caroline, frantically drawing the folds of her negligee around her, knew a moment's terror that the old lady might indeed have lost her reason.

Luis went toward her, his shoulders expressing the grim contrition that had twisted his face as he turned away. Caroline, still at the mercy of her emotions, admired his repossession of control, even while she ached with the awareness of its finality. Whatever happened, they would never have another chance of being alone together; Doña Isabel would see to that. And while she knew she should despise herself for promoting his self-contempt, she *couldn't*. Deep inside her she knew that had Doña Isabel not interrupted them, Luis would not have been capable of denying her, and once they had been lovers, surely he could not then have turned away. He was not meant for a life of celibacy. Whatever promises his mother had dragged from him, he was a man first, not a priest, and her nails dug into her palms as his aunt delivered her incomprehensible tirade.

"It is all right, *tía*," Luis interrupted her at last, raising his hand in a gesture of defeat. He glanced bleakly toward Caroline, and she saw indeed that what she had feared had happened. "I lost my head, that is all." His mouth compressed, and he looked back at his aunt. "Do not look so shocked, *tía*. It will never happen again."

"The girl is leaving?" It was a statement rather than a question, delivered in English as her accusations had not been, and Luis inclined his head.

"Tomorrow," he agreed flatly. "You will arrange for Tomas to take her?"

Doña Isabel looked venomously at Caroline. "I will

arrange it," she agreed and, turning, stalked haughtily away.

"Luis—"

Almost as soon as his aunt had disappeared from her sight, Caroline whispered his name, taking a step toward him appealingly, putting out her hands in mute supplication. But Luis's face was stark and cold.

"Goodbye," he said, and his voice was as chilling as his appearance. "My aunt is right. You are a danger— to all of us!"

Caroline quivered. "Is that what she said?"

"In essence," he agreed heavily. "*Adiós, señorita. ¡Mucha suerte!*"

"Luis!"

She said his name again, but he had gone, and she was left speaking to an empty room. She said his name many times after she had crawled into the opulent luxury of the bed, but nothing, and no one, could assuage her grief.

SHE PACKED HER BAGS before breakfast, and by the time Carmencita brought her tray, she had them safely stowed in the bathroom. The last thing she wanted was to draw attention to her departure, and knowing how the servants talked, she intended to behave just as if nothing unusual was about to happen.

She had not slept after Luis's departure. Her eyes felt sticky and her head ached, but she managed to drink two cups of coffee as a restorative, and was tense and apprehensive when a knock came at her door.

It was Doña Isabel as she was used to seeing her, bedecked in all her finery, jewels glittering on every finger, her headdress coiled above heavy gold earrings. If her eyes still glittered with the same malevolent light they had shown the night before, Caroline chose not to see them, inclining her head and listening politely to what the old lady had to say.

"You will conduct lessons with Emilia as usual this morning, *señorita*," she announced bleakly, causing

Caroline to look up in surprise. "Well," she continued, "you do not wish for your departure to be made public, do you, *señorita*? Is it not simpler to leave this afternoon, while the. . .household is taking siesta?"

After she had recovered from the immediate shock of knowing she was not leaving immediately, Caroline had to concede that the plan had some merit. "Will—will you tell Emilia goodbye for me, *señora*?" she ventured tautly. "I—I regret—disappointing her like this. Please ask her to forgive me."

"Emilia will soon forget you, *señorita*," retorted Doña Isabel without sympathy. "Sooner or later my nephew will marry again, and when he does, Emilia will learn to love her stepmother."

"Yes, *señora*."

Caroline spoke politely, but although she expected the old lady to leave her, Doña Isabel lingered a little longer.

"Why did you have to corrupt Luis?" she demanded suddenly, staring at the girl with those wild accusing eyes. "He was a man, not like his brother, but you tried to destroy him!"

"That's not true!" Caroline's face was burning, but she managed to answer her. "Luis—I—it was inevitable. I didn't cause it to happen. It just did."

Doña Isabel snorted contemptuously. "You expect me to believe that?"

"Yes." Caroline sought for words to defend herself. "Why—why you yourself accused him of having a woman in the village!"

"*¡Quia!* What nonsense is this?"

"You did. You did." Caroline linked and unlinked her fingers. "That night. . .at dinner. The night you complained to Don Esteban about the woman using the—the *puerta accessoria*—"

"Pah! Stupid girl!" Doña Isabel's lips curled. "Did you really believe I was accusing Luis?" She shook her head. "No. No, do you hear me? I pretended because that was what Esteban wanted me to believe.

But I knew the woman came not to see Luis, but to see him.''

"Maria Pascale?" whispered Caroline faintly, and Doña Isabel looked taken aback.

"That is her name!" she granted harshly. "How do you know? Who told you? Not Esteban?"

"No. Luis," replied Caroline, hardly understanding any of this. "Then. . . who is she?"

"You do not know? Luis did not tell you that?"

"Luis? No." Caroline shook her head. "Please—"

"Maria Pascale is his mother's sister's daughter!" spat Doña Isabel venomously.

"His cousin?"

"And Esteban's mistress!" announced the old lady scornfully. "To save her family from being ejected from the pitiful holding that is all Esteban allows them!"

Caroline shook her head. "I—I can't believe it."

"Why not? Did not Luis explain why he is obliged to remain at the seminary? Did not tell you of his brother's threats concerning his mother and her family?"

"No!" But a faint light was dawning. "You mean, Esteban owns—everything?"

But Doña Isabel was turning away, her face twisted as if she suspected she had said too much. And yet as Caroline allowed what the woman had said to filter into her consciousness, she was left with the certain knowledge that as far as she was concerned, Luis was as remote from her as ever.

Emilia must have thought she was rather grumpy that morning, answering only when she was spoken to, conducting the lessons without her usual good humor. It was as well that Juanita and Victor were still absent. She did not think she could have handled an argumentative group.

Esteban did not appear for lunch, but Emilia volunteered the information that the doctor had visited the hacienda again that morning. "They say he still has a fever," she remarked indifferently. "Are you going to see him, *señorita*? To apologize for leaving him to walk all the way home?"

"No." Caroline's answer was too abrupt, and she qualified it hastily. It would not do to rouse any suspicions now. "Your father left me, Emilia. I was expected to walk home. It wasn't my fault that he overturned the carriage."

"Or that you got a ride home with Giulio and his friends," remarked Emilia. "Oh, yes. I know about that. Benito told me. Benito is a good friend. He tells me everything."

Caroline acknowledged this, and to her relief, Emilia's nursemaid appeared a few moments later to take the child for her rest. But as the little girl left her, Caroline put out her hand and touched her cheek.

"Goodbye, Emilia," she said, forcing a faint smile to her lips, and Emilia pulled a face.

"Hasta la vista, señorita," she responded, and Caroline nodded her head because she didn't trust herself to speak.

Her cases were brought downstairs and taken out to the Range Rover, and then Doña Isabel accompanied her to the top of the flight of steps. Although it was fine at the moment, and humid, too, it had been raining and a faint mist was rising from the ground. This was how she would remember it, thought Caroline tremulously, the warmth, and the color, and the damp smells of the garden—and Luis's face, fatigued by the tensions of suppressed passion.

Tomas stowed her bags into the back of the Range Rover and then joined her inside, seating himself behind the wheel. He seemed narrow eyed and jumpy, and Caroline wondered why, but as he spoke no English she looked forward to a silent journey.

Gomez opened the gates as they drove through, raising his battered hat as they passed, and Caroline's throat tightened. She had come here with such high hopes. Now they had all been dashed and she was leaving like a stranger in the night. Only it wasn't night, and she was no stranger; only a half-frightened girl caught in a trap she had scarcely apprehended.

After the rain of the past days, the ground under the vehicle's wheels was waterlogged and heavy, and the journey down to the village was a hair-raising one. Even going downhill, the wheels skidded to the edge of the road, spinning uselessly over ditches before regaining purchase on the slippery ground Caroline clung helplessly to her seat, trying not to watch Tomas too closely, but she couldn't help seeing how the Mexican's sweating hands had difficulty in holding onto the wheel.

About a mile beyond the village, Tomas suddenly changed his tactics, pulling his vehicle off the road into a belt of trees. Caroline thought at first he was stopping to recover his nerve, but to her surprise he glanced at her and said, *"¡Perdone me, señorita!"* and then thrust open his door and climbed out. Within seconds he had disappeared, running as if for his life through the trees.

Caroline was stunned, as much by Tomas's uncharacteristic attitude as by any immediate fear for herself. What was wrong with the man? Hadn't he the nerve to drive her to Las Estadas? Perhaps he suspected that Esteban did not know of her departure and was alarmed that he might be blamed.

Caroline shook her head. Surely Doña Isabel had explained. Surely he understood that he was simply following orders. If Esteban was angry, his censure would fall on his daughter and his aunt, and Caroline knew a pang of remorse when she thought of Emilia's reactions to her disappearance.

Still, her most immediate need was to get to Las Estadas. If she drove the range Rover, Tomas would have a difficult time explaining; but if that was the only way, she would have to do it.

This thought had barely surfaced when she heard footsteps coming through the trees, and she expelled her breath in relief. Of course. Why hadn't she thought of that? Tomas had stopped for the most natural reason in the world, and had she been more premature and driven away without him, he would surely have been very angry.

A smile forming on her lips at her own foolishness, she turned—only to feel the smile freezing on her lips like a grimace. It was not Tomas who swung open the door of the Range Rover and climbed in beside her, but Esteban. For several blank seconds she could neither move nor articulate.

"Ah, *señorita*!" As he lounged into the seat beside her, he was smiling beneficently. "Did you think to leave without saying goodbye? Shame on you, Miss Leyton?"

CHAPTER ELEVEN

IT WAS WITH AN EFFORT that Caroline regained her composure. "What—what are you doing here, *señor*?" she asked, trying to appear calm and unperturbed by his appearance. "I thought Tomas was driving me to Las Estadas." There was no point in pretending she had been going anywhere else, with her suitcases plainly visible in the back of the vehicle. "I thought you were ill, *señor*."

"A cold, nothing more." Esteban dismissed his condition with a careless wave of his hand, but Caroline could see it had been a little more than that. Whether he was cured, she could not be sure, but certainly something had left dark rings around his eyes and robbed his sallow face of all color. "So now," he continued, firing the ignition, "let us get on. It would not do for you to miss your bus, would it?"

And to have to spend another night at the inn, Caroline reflected uneasily, finishing what had been implicit in Esteban's statement. She wondered how on earth he had learned she was leaving.

The Range Rover squelched out from the trees onto the road again, and Caroline half expected Esteban to turn back the way they had come. She couldn't believe he had arrived just to drive her to Las Estadas. It didn't make sense, and it was certainly out of character. But they turned away from San Luis on the road that led through the semitropical terrain that lay between them and Las Estadas, and Caroline expelled her breath unevenly, wondering what, if anything, he intended to do with her. There were quite a few miles between San Luis and Las Estadas, areas of jungle and vegetation, in which a person could disappear and never be found again. Within weeks her bones would be picked dry by the predators that roamed the forest, and her whole body broke out in a cold sweat at the thought of such a fate.

"You seem...dismayed, *señorita*," Esteban remarked suddenly, breaking in on her morbid thoughts, causing her to look at him apprehensively. "Why should the idea of my driving you to Las Estadas worry you so much? We have driven this way before."

Caroline's tongue circled her dry lips. "Why didn't you drive me from the hacienda then, *señor*? Why didn't you tell your aunt that you would take me to Las Estadas?"

"But I did." Esteban sounded quite put out, and Caroline stared at him disbelievingly. "It is true," he persisted. "It was I who suggested you leave after lunch. I am afraid I had an appointment with the doctor this morning, and therefore it was impossible for me to get away."

Caroline could not comprehend what he was saying. "Your aunt—Doña Isabel *knew*?"

"But of course." Esteban half smiled. Tía Isabel tells me everything. Did you not know?"

"No." Caroline's response was barely audible. But at least she now knew how Esteban had found out she was leaving. Did he also know about Luis's visit the night before?

"I insisted on taking you myself," Esteban added now. "It was the least I could do after our last...confrontation. But I had business in the village, and I suggested Tomas bring you on the first stage of the journey and meet me here." He paused to allow another vehicle to pass them, a hazardous venture at the best of times, and doubly so now with the roads slippery and streaming with water. "I wanted to apologize," he went on. "To ask you to forgive my selfish temper."

Caroline would have thought his behavior had had more serious overtones than a mere flash of temper implied, but his explanations were relieving her so much that she was prepared to believe almost anything just to get the journey over. Afterward she would consider why Tomas should have apologized to her as he got out of the vehicle; why he should have stopped in such a remote spot to change drivers; and why Doña Isabel, who had pretended to be helping her, should have reported all her doings to her nephew. But for now she acknowledged his apology with a forced smile, and crossed her fingers tightly as the Range Rover turned a corner a little too fast and skidded to the edge of the track.

"So—" Esteban glanced her way "—you are feeling better now, *señorita*? You do not think Esteban is such a villain, after all?"

Caroline shook her head. "I—I never thought you were a villain, *señor*."

"No?" He sounded skeptical. "But you would rather believe my brother than me, no?"

Caroline caught her lower lip between her teeth. "I beg your pardon?"

"Luis. You believe everything Luis has told you."

"He has told me nothing, *señor*."

"No?" Esteban blatantly did not believe her, and the feeling of unease rekindled inside her. "He did not tell you that, like Tía Isabel, my mother was a little—how shall I put it—unusual?"

"No." Caroline spoke firmly this time. "Why should he tell me that? Your—your aunt is as sane as you or I."

"Hmm." Esteban absorbed this while Caroline's pulse fluttered a little faster. "Nevertheless, it has to be said that my mother was a little strange. Of course, Tía Isabel believes that my father was responsible for her condition. He was... fond of women, *señorita*. He had many mistresses."

Caroline did not make any response. She hoped that if she said nothing he would eventually grow tired of baiting her, but she should have known that Esteban enjoyed the pursuit as much as the capture.

"Of course," he continued, "after mama was dead, and he married Luis's mother, he became a model husband. I did not know what Irena had, but she kept him home at nights, and for that I should admire her." He laughed at this, and then broke off to cough rather hoarsely as the legacy of the chill he had taken racked his lungs. "Luis, of course, was the apple of her eye, but not of my father's, obviously. Else why did he leave the estate to me, and nothing to his wife's precious bastard!"

"Luis is not a bastard!" Caroline could keep silent no longer. "He—he's just as much your father's son as you are. And—and it is unfair that the estate should not be divided."

"Ah, yes." Esteban glanced at her again, his gaze more speculative now, and Caroline wished he would keep his eyes on the road. It was too precarious a route to treat so contemptuously, and the adrenaline pumped through her veins as they careered across the road, narrowly missing an enormous pothole.

"I suppose Luis told you what happened to his mother after my father died?"

Caroline hesitated. "He told me she entered a convent, yes."

"Yes. A convent." Esteban's lips curled. "She knew I would not allow her to stay at San Luis, so she took the easy way out, eh?"

Caroline moved her shoulders helplessly. "It's nothing to do with me, *señor*."

Esteban shrugged. "She thought she was so clever."

"Clever, *señor*?" Caroline was confused.

"Yes, clever," repeated Esteban harshly. "She knew I hated her. And Luis. She knew that once papa was dead I would do anything in my power to get rid of them." He sneered. "She thought that by entering the convent she had thwarted me." He laughed again, but it was not a pleasant sound and Caroline shivered. "She thought Luis would be more than a match for me. But she had forgotten about the rest of her family."

"The rest of her family?" Caroline couldn't help the involuntary question, and he nodded.

"The Pascales. They live on the estate. They were my father's tenants. How else do you think he met Luis's mother?" His mouth twisted. "Peasants, all of them! Unfit to mingle their blood with ours!"

Caroline was beginning to understand. Doña Isabel had spoken of the Pascales. Of Luis's cousin Maria. But where did Luis come in?

"My father had Luis educated, of course," Esteban continued now. "For a peasant, he is remarkably intelligent."

Caroline's nails dug painfully into her palms, but she kept silent. He went on, "My father sent him to university in California. He gained a degree in agricultural studies. To help my father run the estate, you understand?"

Caroline nodded, not trusting herself to speak, and Esteban went on with his monologue.

"He came home with many...radical ideas. Ideas about social conditions, and democratizing the rights of the peons." He shook his head. "My father pretended to listen to him. He even agreed to try some of his methods. But fortunately a seizure robbed him of the power to speak or move, and he was a living vegetable until his death."

Caroline caught her breath. "He was your father!"

"He was not fit to be my father at the end. He had destroyed everything my family ever stood for. He had mingled the blood of conquistadores with that of slaves, and he deserved to die!"

Caroline shook her head. "And—and afterward?" She had to know.

"Afterward, as I said, Luis's mother entered the convent. She thought she had won. That Luis would stay here at the hacienda and share the running of the estate. She knew he was stronger than I was. That he was not afraid of horses, as I was, and that the men would be loyal to him." He smiled unpleasantly. "But unfortunately she had forgotten Luis is also an honorable man. When I put it to him that his mother's family might fare badly if they were deprived of their small holding, he understood. Particularly as he knew that being forced to leave their home would kill his aunt and uncle."

Caroline's lips trembled. "Why are you telling me all this, *señor*?"

"I thought you would like to know," remarked Esteban airily. "Just in case you had any foolish ideas that Luis might come after you." He shook his head. "Luis will not betray his family, *señorita*, and after all, why should he for a harlot such as you?"

Caroline flinched as if he had struck her. And she supposed that like a snake he had. He had destroyed any hopes she might have nurtured that Luis might change his mind, and finally bestowed upon her an ugly epithet such as he had previously reserved for Luis's mother. She had been right to feel afraid of him, to be apprehensive of the outcome of this journey. He had insulted her and abused her, and she felt as unclean as his words had made her.

"Have you nothing to say in your own defense, *señorita*?" he taunted now. She saw to her relief that they were nearing the outskirts of Las Estadas. The journey was almost over, and she could hardly wait to be free of him.

"Well?" he persisted. "Is it not true that you have a lover in England? A lover, moreover, who already has a wife?"

Caroline stiffened, and then, realizing that Doña Isabel must have told him this, also, she straightened her spine and answered him. "I have no lovers, *señor*," she declared coldly. "Unlike your pitiful aunt and her sister, and Señorita Calveiro, I find more satisfaction in books and learning than in prostrating myself before some ignorant macho!"

Esteban sucked in his breath. "Have a care, *señorita*. You are not in England yet. And a woman like you should welcome any man's attentions!"

Caroline refused to look at him, even while the blood was pounding through her head, and apprehension overwhelmed her previous recklessness. Yet what could he do now, she argued with herself as the shabby streets of Las Estadas engulfed them—but could find no comfort in the fateful question.

The bus station, she knew, was at the far side of the town, a corrugated-roofed building with a small office for booking tickets. The bus service in Mexico was surprisingly good, and although the trip from Mérida to Las Estadas had been a tiring journey, Caroline had not found it uncomfortable. Now, however, she didn't much care whether the coming trip was comfortable or not. She just wanted to escape from Esteban's company and the cruel crudity of his tongue.

Esteban did not take the main road through the town. He turned left into a narrower street lined with closely packed houses and smelling of stale food and unwashed humanity. Caroline was not immediately dismayed. She thought it might be a more direct route to the bus station. She still had to ascertain that there was transport out of Las Estadas this evening, but surely Doña Isabel would not have let her come without being sure. And then she remembered that Doña Isabel was not to be trusted, and Luis had expected her to leave that morning.

Fear feathered over her skin like a cobweb's touch. The truth was, she was putting her faith in a man who had professed to despise her. She already knew what he was like. She had no need to doubt the flaws in his character. And remembering the butterfly, she wondered if she had any more chance of escaping unscathed.

When Esteban brought the Range Rover to a halt beside a pair of ramshackle wooden gates, her heart almost stopped beating. This was definitely not the bus station. She glanced at him anxiously, trying to hide her fear.

"Where are we?" she asked, trying to remain cool. "What is this place? Why have we stopped here?"

Esteban smiled, but the mobility of his mouth did not reach his eyes. They were still as hard and calculating as ever, and Caroline felt the sweat break out on her palms. "One moment, *señorita*," he told her lightly, pushing open his door and climbing down from the cab. "I have some small business to attend to. I will join you shortly!" And slamming the door behind him, he sauntered through the sagging gates.

Caroline could hardly stop her knees from shaking. Specks of rain splattered the windscreen, and the sky had grown darker, casting gloomy shadows down the main street. Where was she, she wondered, too conscious of her own vulnerability to try to investigate. If only she understood the language, she thought desperately. But it was too late now to wish something like that.

Another van stopped behind them, and glancing around, she saw two men unloading some crates. Their contents appeared to be bottles of some sort, and she watched them half idly, still absorbed with her own problems. It was only when they pushed the wooden gates wide and she could see the back of the building that comprehension dawned. It was the inn, she could swear it. The men were carrying in crates of beer and tequila. And as if to confirm this, Esteban emerged from the building at that moment accompanied by Señor Allende. He was gesturing toward the Range Rover as he spoke, evidently unaware that she could see them, but judging by the malicious amusement that his words were engendering, her own predicament was being discussed.

Panic flared inside her. If Esteban was speaking to the innkeeper, a man whom previously he had despised, he had to have an ulterior motive. And she did not need a crystal ball to guess what he intended.

Battening down the hysteria that threatened to overwhelm her, she acted purely on instinct. Esteban had left the keys in the ignition, obviously never expecting her to touch them, but now she levered herself across

the central console into the driver's seat and turned the
ignition switch.

Esteban saw her as the engine fired, but although he
broke into a run, with the fat little proprietor at his
heels, they were much too late to stop her. She released
the clutch at the same time as she pressed down hard on
the accelerator, and the vehicle practically leaped forward. A giggle of hysteria escaped her as she careered
wildly down the street.

She had no idea which way the bus station lay. She
drove purely on instinct, as she had done everything
else. But fate, or the gods—call it what you will—must
have been on her side, for as she emerged into the main
street again she saw the roof of the bus station only a
few yards ahead of her.

She guessed Esteban would follow her, but she had to
risk it. Somehow, it didn't matter how, she was taking a
bus out of Las Estadas tonight, and she didn't much
care where it took her.

AN HOUR LATER, seated on the bus to Mérida, she
reviewed the events leading up to her departure with a
sense of incredulity. As she'd expected, Esteban had
come after her, but for once the fact that she was
English had proved a blessing. Waiting at the bus station, for the very bus she wanted to board, was a party
of British tourists who had been spending three days
visiting archaeological sites in the area, and hearing
their familiar voices, she had quickly introduced herself.
Her explanation that she had taken a job in the area that
hadn't worked out evoked some raised eyebrows among
the older ladies of the group, but her smile, which felt
glued to her face, was so appealing that they were forced
to believe her.

Esteban arrived, hot and irate, as they were boarding
the streamlined vehicle that was to take them to Mérida.
Señor Allende was still with him, panting to keep up
with Esteban's longer stride, and Caroline suspected it
was to him she owed her freedom. Alone Esteban might

have had some credibility, but with the fat, perspiring little proprietor beside him, he assumed an air of seedy respectability that was not at all convincing. His story that Caroline was leaving his employ without gaining permission or giving notice was received with tight-lipped disapproval, and it was soon obvious that the ladies of the party thought Caroline had had a lucky escape. Esteban's imperious attitude did not impress them, and they grew quite indignant on her behalf when he threatened her with legal action.

"I suggest you take it up with the consulate," suggested one elderly female, viewing the innkeeper's sweat-streaked face with distaste. "I am sure they will be quite willing to help you, if you feel some compensation is necessary."

"Oh, yes." Esteban's mouth twisted as he watched Caroline climb aboard the bus. "I shall have compensation, *señora*. You can be assured of that!" And as he strode away, Caroline realized that someone else would pay for this afternoon's work.

She hoped it would not be Emilia. Remembering the child as she had last seen her, her heart ached terribly. But what could she do, she asked herself despairingly. Esteban held all the cards, and she could only blame his father for the unjust terms of his will. If he had cared for Luis's mother, as he must have done to marry her and remain faithful to her, why had he not kept faith with their child?

Esteban and Luis should have shared the estate—any honorable man would have known that. But Esteban was not an honorable man; he was coarse and insensitive, vindictive to the point of cruelty, and incapable of inspiring anything but bitterness and fear in the people who served him.

CHAPTER TWELVE

THERE WAS AN AUTUMN CHILL IN THE AIR as Caroline walked home from the station. Already the summer was over, and the previous night's wind had brought a showering of gold and amber leaves to cover the grass. It would be October soon, the start of the university year, but for her there were no new beginnings.

She had managed to find a job at a travel agency. It was not really the kind of occupation she wanted, but all the teaching vacancies had been filled by now. Besides, she had not yet decided that teaching was what she wanted to do, either.

Somehow, since her return from Mexico four weeks ago, she had found it almost impossible to settle into anything. What had once absorbed her now seemed only faintly interesting, and the idea of going on and furthering her career had lost its initial spark. How amused Esteban would be if he knew, she thought bitterly, unable to dispel the images that persistently tormented her mind. She, the quintessential career girl, would have given everything she possessed to be one man's wife....

Luis! She thrust her hands more deeply into the pockets of her creamy leather jacket, feeling the familiar weakness the thought of him evoked. She wondered if he ever thought of her in his lonely monastic cell, or whether time and separation had achieved for him what could not be achieved for her. Perhaps his religion was enough. Perhaps it was sufficient compensation. But for her there was only pain and emptiness, and the certain knowledge that this time there was no escape.

Seeing Andrew again had not helped. She had wondered whether meeting him again would bring any of the old excitement his presence used to generate, but it hadn't worked. He was like an old friend, nothing more, and she was glad she had never permitted their relationship to extend beyond the bounds of a tender flirtation. She liked him. She supposed she always would. And certainly she sympathized with the difficulties he experienced in his marriage. But her own feelings for him had fallen into perspective, and what she had imagined to be love had been merely hero worship.

Now she crossed the square and turned into the quiet mews where her parents' house was situated. It was early evening, and already the shadows were casting pools of darkness between the burgeoning illumination of the streetlamps. Soon it would be dark before she left the office and the real winter nights would begin, nights when she would have more than enough time to fear the future and regret the past.

There were lights already in her parents' house, flooding out over the neatly painted window boxes that her mother tended with such care. The cobbled court before the house was occupied by her father's shabby Rover, which he refused to part with despite her mother's urgings, and the doors to the garage had been opened to reveal her mother's smarter Mini. That her father hadn't immediately put the Rover into the garage was a source of wonder to her, and she guessed something must have happened to interrupt his usual routine.

Without feeling any real sense of apprehension she inserted her key into the lock and entered the house as usual, calling out a greeting to her mother as she hung her coat in the hall. As far as she was concerned, she was glad to be home, and the warm sense of security it gave her wrapped itself around her like a second skin. Her parents had never interfered in her life, and they had accepted her explanation that the job in Mexico hadn't worked out with only a degree of speculation.

But now, when her mother emerged into the hall to confront her, there was a definite look of anticipation on her face. Caroline felt her own color falter when Mrs. Leyton hastily closed the sitting-room door behind her.

"You have a visitor," she said at once in an under-tone. "Two visitors, in fact. Señor de Montejo and—and Emilia!"

Caroline groped weakly for the banister. "Did—did you say—Señor de Montejo?"

"That's right." Her mother wrung her hands awk-wardly. "You'd better come in. Your father's just of-fered him a drink, but I think you ought to come and speak to him." She paused. "He...well, he wants you to go back and take up your teaching job again, and when I told him you were not likely to agree, he said he hoped he'd be able to make you change your mind."

Caroline was trembling. She had never expected this to happen. When she had left Esteban at the bus station, she had known he was angry, but she had never dreamed he would follow her to London, or involve her parents in his sordid affairs.

"I—I don't want to see him," she said now, glancing around her anxiously. "Oh, mum, I really don't want to see him."

"Why not?" Her mother looked at her reprovingly. "Caroline, I really think you ought to. He has traveled all this way. Don't you think it's the least you can do?"

"No—"

"Caroline, be reasonable—"

"I am being reasonable." Caroline could feel the panic rising inside her. "I—I—it's four weeks since I left Mexico. If—if he was so keen to retain my services, he should have contacted me before I got another job."

"Well, apparently his brother died—" began Mrs. Leyton thoughtfully, marshaling her argument, and then exclaimed, "Caroline! Oh, dear heaven!" as her daughter slumped in a dead faint at the foot of the stairs.

"Do YOU THINK I should call the doctor?"

Caroline came round to the sound of her mother's voice speaking softly somewhere nearby, but when her eyes opened, it was not either of her parents who was gazing down at her.

"Luis?" she breathed, convinced she must be dreaming. Then, more strongly, "Luis, what are you doing here?" as he came down on the side of the couch on which she was lying.

"*Saludos, pequeña*," he murmured softly, laying one of his hands over both of hers where they were pressed together at her midriff. "I did not realize my arrival would be so traumatic for you." He paused, his gray eyes dark with emotion. "Would you prefer that we leave and come back later?"

"No—"

Caroline's involuntary denial, and her feeble attempt to struggle up from the pillows, attracted her parents' attention. They had been talking quietly together near the sitting-room door, but now they turned and gazed anxiously at her and at the man toward whom she was gazing so eagerly.

But it was someone else who interrupted them, someone small and dark and excited, dressed more suitably than Caroline had ever seen her, in a pretty fringed suede skirt and jacket and a simple woolen sweater.

"*Señorita, señorita!*" she exclaimed, jumping up from the chair on which she had been sitting as soon as she saw that Caroline was conscious. "*Señorita*, we have come to take you back to San Luis with us. Say you will come, please say you will come. Tío Vincente so much wants you to live with us."

Caroline could only shake her head, staring at Emilia as if she couldn't believe her eyes, and this time Luis intervened, drawing Emilia to his side with a gentle insistence, raising his finger warningly as she started to protest.

"It is too soon," he assured her quietly as Caroline glanced around at her mother and father, wondering how they were taking all this. "Miss Leyton got quite a shock to find us here. I think we should go away now and leave her to recover."

"No!" Caroline's voice was firmer as she clutched at Luis's hand. "No, please—" She cast another imploring glance at her parents. "I mean, I have got over it. I am all right, honestly." She struggled into a sitting position, gazing at him wonderingly. "Luis, please—tell me why you are here."

"You know that already," put in Mrs. Leyton dryly, crossing the floor to the couch and looking down at her daughter with half-impatient eyes. "Caroline, I told you what Señor de Montejo had said. But you refused to see him. Do I take it now that you have changed your mind?"

"She was shocked, Elizabeth." Caroline's father joined the group around the couch. "How are you feeling, darling? I've never known you to pass out like that before."

"I'm fine, daddy." Caroline was clinging to Luis's hand as if she would never let him go, and her parents exchanged helpless glances. "I—I didn't know you meant—Luis, you see."

"I think we've gathered that, Caroline," her mother responded dryly. "I suppose it was my fault. I should have explained. But how was I to know you were likely to react so violently?"

Caroline shook her head, looking at Luis urgently. "She—she said you—your brother is dead. Is that true?" She caught her lower lip between her teeth as she met Emilia's dark eyes. "I—I can hardly believe it."

"There was a car crash." It was Emilia who spoke. "On the way back from Las Estadas. Señor Allende was driving, but the roads were slippery—"

"What?" Caroline gasped, and her returning color receded again. "Luis... do you mean—"

"I think we ought to leave them alone, Elizabeth." Mr. Leyton could sense the tenseness of the atmosphere,

and Caroline's mother pulled herself together and nodded in agreement.

"Yes. Yes. I—I'll make some tea," she said. And
then, glancing at Emilia, she added, "Would you like to
come and help me, young lady? I think your uncle
would prefer to speak with—with Caroline alone."

Emilia looked doubtful, but Luis finally extracted his
hand from Caroline's and rose firmly to his feet. "I
think that is a very good idea, Emilia," he averred, pro-
pelling her gently away from him. "Miss Leyton and I
do have some private matters to discuss. Perhaps Mrs.
Leyton will let you pour out the milk for her while her
daughter and I discuss the possibilities of her returning
to Mexico with us, hmm?"

"You won't go away?"

Obviously, for all her apparent indifference to her
father's death, Emilia was still very much a child, and as
a child she craved security. Luis shook his head.

"I promise I shall be here all the time," he assured
her softly. "Thank you." This to Caroline's mother. "I
am most grateful."

Caroline's mother made a deprecating gesture and
then ushered Emilia ahead of her out of the room. Mr.
Leyton closed the door behind them, and the silence
that followed their departure was broken only by Caroline's unsteady breathing.

"Esteban is dead," she whispered, still hardly able to
believe it. "Because—because of me—"

"Of course not." Luis turned to face her tautly.
"Tomas was to take you to Las Estadas, and I hazard a
guess that Tomas would not have turned the car off the
road. Esteban was drunk, and so was Allende, as far as
we can gather. He must have been to have attempted the
journey in that condition."

Caroline shook her head. "It doesn't seem possible."

"Why?" Luis paced restlessly across the hearth and
back again. "Because of what he threatened you with?
Because you were afraid it was he, and not me, who had
come to find you?"

Caroline swung her legs to the floor, pushing back her hair with an unsteady hand. "How—how do you know about that?"

"How do you think?" Luis made a sound of impatience. "Where do you think they did their drinking? At the hotel, of course. There are a dozen witnesses there willing to say that Esteban threatened you with beating, raping and worse!" His dark face was grim. "God knows what he might have done had he reached San Luis alive. One thing is certain: Emilia and Tía Isabel would have borne the brunt of his fury."

Caroline's tongue circled her lips as she looked up at him. "How— how did you find out?"

"About what? The fact that your departure had been delayed—or Esteban's accident?"

Caroline frowned. "Well—the accident, I suppose."

"I arrived on the scene only minutes after it had happened," Luis retorted curtly. As she gazed at him incredulously, he went on, "It was Emilia who told me what had happened."

"Emilia?"

"Yes." Luis nodded. "You see, you had not told her you were leaving, but when she visited her friend Benito, that afternoon, he confided what had happened."

"A—about Esteban?"

"But of course. By then Tomas had come back, and the servants knew what was going on. It was a source of excitement to them that the *patron* should get up from his sickbed to follow the young English lady to Las Estadas."

"But Emilia—"

Luis sighed, spreading his hands. "She thought he had dismissed you. You know how her imagination works. She was afraid, but for different reasons."

"And she sent for you?"

"Tomas reluctantly agreed to call at the seminary."

Caroline shook her head. "And?"

Luis made a sound of self-derision. "*Dios mio*, you

can have no idea how I felt when I heard what had happened.''

Caroline got rather falteringly to her feet. "He—he might have had the best of intentions.''

Luis bent his head. "He might. But I had to be sure." He thrust his hands behind his back, and she could see the tautness of his muscles beneath the fine cloth. "I was afraid—I was afraid that he—''

"Might touch me?" she ventured softly, and he nodded.

"Did he?"

"No." She shook her head again and quickly explained what had happened. "I don't know what I'd have done without the others," she admitted, mentioning the tourist party she had joined. "They—they were very kind to me. I flew back to London with them.''

"Thank God for that." Luis's thanks were heartfelt.

Caroline managed a faint smile. "When—when my mother told me he—he was dead, I thought—I thought at first—''

"She meant me?" Luis finished for her, and she inclined her head.

"That's why I fainted, I suppose. All—all the blood just seemed to drain out of me.''

"Oh, Caroline!"

With a groan of impatience he filled the space between them, stepping so close to her that she almost lost her balance and collapsed onto the couch again.

"It is too soon, is it not?" he breathed, his dark jacket brushing the swollen fullness of her breasts. "I should not have come here yet. I should have written to you and told you what had happened, begged you in letter form to reconsider your decision.''

"My decision?" Caroline's voice had a tremor, but she didn't try to hide it. "What decision?"

"The decision to come back to us," exclaimed Luis huskily. "We need you.... Emilia needs you—''

"And—and you?" Caroline looked up at him, lifting her hands to finger the smooth satiny hide of his leather jacket. "Do you need me, Luis?" She paused and then added recklessly, "Because—because I need you...."

Her words were cut off by the probing pressure of his mouth. As if whatever willpower he possessed had suddenly snapped, his arms were around her, hauling her closely against him. She could feel every stirring muscle of his body, and the searching possession of his kiss robbed her of what little strength remained in her legs. She sagged against him, shaking with reaction, and he bent to swing her up into his arms, looking down at her with eyes burning with passion.

"I need you," he agreed thickly as she looped her arms round his neck. "And God knows, I have never said that to any woman before."

Caroline pressed her face against his neck. "But the seminary...?"

"I think you know why I entered the seminary," he said heavily, lounging into an armchair with her on his lap. "*Tía* Isabel told you, did she not?"

"And Esteban," said Caroline softly, burrowing against him, parting the lapels of his jacket and nestling against the soft silk of his shirt. "In case I—I imagined you might...come after me."

"Oh, *mi querida*, there was always that possibility." He shook his head. "Each time I saw you it was harder to go back—to go on with the life I had made for myself." He bent his head to nuzzle his lips against her ear. "And when Tómas brought the message that Esteban had taken you to Las Estadas—" He broke off with a sound of anguish. "I knew that whatever happened, my immortal soul was not worth the sacrifice I was making."

"Luis!" She cupped his face between her hands, gazing at him disbelievingly. "You mean—you are not going back? Ever?"

"Did you doubt it?"

"I don't know. I was afraid to believe it." Caroline was so overwhelmed she could hardly speak. "Oh, Luis—I love you so much!"

"¡Cristo!" His tongue probed the hollows of her ear while his hand slid up to cradle her throat. "Can you not feel I am trembling, *querida*? Believe me, I did not come here secure in your love. I was afraid—so afraid—that this man, this man you cared for, might have replaced me completely in your affections."

"Andrew?" Caroline lifted her face to his like a flower seeking the sun. "Oh, Luis, I never loved Andrew. I realized that almost as soon as we met. He—I cared for him, I suppose, but not—not in the way I care for you."

"Dios gracias," muttered Luis fervently before seeking her mouth with his once again.

Their kisses were becoming deeper, more passionate, and as if aware that her parents might intrude upon them at any time, Luis finally dragged himself away to rest his head back against the soft upholstery.

"So," he said, his eyes still drugged and sensual, "you will come back with me?"

"If you want me to," she agreed, loosening his tie and the top two buttons of his shirt, and bestowing a kiss on the brown column of his throat she had exposed. "Hmm, your skin is slightly damp and salty—"

"And overstimulated," he groaned hoarsely, pushing her teasing fingers away. "Caroline, do not push me too far, I beg of you. I would not wish to embarrass your parents."

"How would you do that?" she persisted, carrying his hand to her lips and allowing her tongue to probe his palm, so that with a smothered oath he bent his head and substituted his mouth for his hand.

Her hands slid around his neck, tangling in the thick dark hair that grew down his nape, and she moaned in submission when his hand slid possessively over her thigh.

"Te deseo," he murmured urgently. "I want you, *querida*. But not here. Not like this. Even though you drive me to the edge of distraction!"

Caroline drew back to look at him. "Do you love me?"

"Love you?" He gazed at her half ruefully. "Oh, *pequeña*, loving is such a simple word to describe the way I feel. I adore you, I worship you! And yes, I love you, too, much more than you could ever imagine."

Caroline thought about her next words before saying them. "What—what about—Doña Isabel?"

"What about her?" Luis expelled his breath heavily, trying without too much success to control his emotions. "Oh. . . you mean because she told Esteban what you planned to do?"

"You know about that?"

"But of course. Tía Isabel and I have had some time to talk about the future."

"And?"

"She knows of my feelings for you." He sighed. "It was this, as much as anything, that tipped the balance against you, I am afraid."

Caroline shook her head. "But. . . why?"

Luis stroked her cheek. "The night she sent for me, she was concerned about you, about what Esteban might do to you." He shrugged. "But then later, when she saw us together, her mind became confused, and the memories of what happened to Esteban's mother, her sister, became inextricably entangled with what she had seen. In her mind you were a corrupting influence, and she turned to Esteban because he was there."

Caroline shivered. "She frightened me."

"Do not be alarmed. She is no longer at San Luis. She left a few days after Esteban was buried. She has gone to stay with a friend of Señora Calveiro's, and afterward she plans to return to Spain."

"To Spain?" Caroline was amazed.

"I, too, was surprised," Luis admitted. "But you must remember, Isabel is no relation of mine. She was Esteban's aunt. My addressing her as *tía* was simply a courtesy title. Now that he is dead, she no longer has ties with the hacienda."

Caroline tried to absorb this. "So—so there will be only the three of us?"

"To begin with," agreed Luis dryly, and her cheeks darkened with becoming color. "So long as you do not object to Emilia's presence."

"Object?" Caroline gasped. "How could I object. She has been through so much!"

Luis hesitated. "You mean...Esteban's death?"

"Her father's death, yes."

"Esteban was not her father," Luis told her heavily, and Caroline felt a sudden chill.

"But—but you said—you told me—"

"I told you *I* was not her father," Luis reminded her quietly. "I did not say Esteban was."

"Then—then who...?"

Luis bent his head. "He was a friend of mine, I regret," he conceded quietly. "A visitor to the hacienda at a time when Juana was most unhappy."

"And Esteban knew this?"

"No." Luis sighed. "I think he secretly believed Emilia was his daughter, even though he allowed the fiction that she was mine to go unchallenged."

"But Emilia—"

"Knows the truth. Or, at least, as much of it as it is necessary for her to know at this time."

Caroline sighed. "She so much wanted to be your daughter."

Luis shrugged. "And so she shall be...if you will let her live with us. And when there are other children—" he caressed her eyelids with his lips "—she will be their older sister, hmm?"

"Whatever you say," whispered Caroline softly, and he was bending to kiss her again when the door was peremptorily opened and the subject of their last discussion danced into the room.

"Tío Vincente! *Señorita*—oh!" This as Caroline scrambled up rather inelegantly from Luis's knee. Then, her lips quivering a little as she sought to be grown-up about it, "You are going to marry Tío Vincente, after all!"

"If he'll have me," Caroline agreed huskily, and

bent to hug the little girl close to her as Luis accepted.

THREE MONTHS LATER, Caroline returned home from Mariposa one morning to find her husband at work in his study as usual. Since Esteban's death much of the work that had previously fallen on the estate manager's shoulders was now shared by the master of the estate, and the desk that Caroline had always found so empty of any correspondence was now much in use and littered with files and papers.

"Well?" Luis said, getting to his feet as she came into the room and coming around to put his hands on her shoulders. "What did old Rivera say? Tell me at once. Is it what you suspected? *Nombre de Dios* do not keep me in suspense! I have done no work this morning, waiting for your return. You should have let me come with you."

"To hear that you are going to become a father in the near future?" remarked Caroline teasingly, looking up at him.

Luis's gray eyes narrowed. "Then it is true?"

"It seems like it," Caroline nodded.

"Cristo!" Luis gazed down at her half impatiently. "I knew I should have taken more care."

"Why?" Caroline challenged him quietly. "I didn't want you to." She touched his belt suggestively. "I want your baby, Luis. I want us to have lots of babies."

Luis's lean hands stilled her probing fingers. "Caroline, be serious!" he exclaimed, even though his breathing had quickened in concert with hers. "We have not even had a honeymoon yet!"

"We can have one afterward," said Caroline casually. "You know mummy and daddy said they would like to come out here to visit. They can come after the baby is born, and we'll go away together, just the two of us." She sighed ecstatically. "Oh, Emilia's going to be so excited!"

"Caroline, are you sure? Sure you want this baby, I mean?"

"Of course, I'm sure." Caroline pressed herself against him. "Hmm, darling, you look tired. You're working too hard."

"And getting too little sleep," he agreed dryly, and her cheeks dimpled.

"Do you mind?" she murmured, and his eyes darkened with emotion.

"Caroline—"

"Love me," she breathed against his mouth, and with a groan Luis gave in to the temptation of her softly parted lips.

Sometime later, in the twilit luxury of their bedroom, Luis levered himself up on one elbow to look down at the lissome beauty of his wife beside him. Feeling his eyes upon her, Caroline stirred sensuously, in no way embarrassed by his scrutiny. She was completely uninhibited in his presence—he had taught her to be that way—and she loved these moments in the aftermath of lovemaking, when he was so completely hers.

"I had some news myself this morning," he murmured as she lifted her hand to stroke a caressing finger down his chest. "That rogue Vaquera rang me."

"Vaquera?" Caroline frowned. "Isn't he your solicitor or something?"

"He was my father's lawyer, and subsequently Esteban's," Luis agreed, bending to touch her shoulder with his lips. "As far as being mine is concerned, perhaps now he would like to be so."

"Why? What do you mean?" Caroline moved her shoulder against his mouth with sensuous pleasure. "What did he tell you?"

"Only that he had come across my father's last will and testament," Luis informed her dryly, and smiled at her sudden arousal.

"Your father's last will and testament!" she echoed. "You mean—there was a will involving you?"

"Apparently." Luis subsided onto the pillows beside her again, putting a possessive hand on her still flat stomach. "He says it must have been drawn up by one of the junior partners who has since left his employ, but my own opinion is that Esteban had been paying him to keep quiet."

Caroline jackknifed into a sitting position, one leg drawn up to support her chin. "You mean, Esteban was bribing him to keep the will to himself?"

"Something like that," agreed Luis with a shrug. Then, "Come here! It's nothing to get so steamed up about."

"It is so." Caroline was indignant. "Do you realize what this means?"

"It means that I now legally own from my father something I previously owned on my brother's death," observed Luis quietly. His eyes darkened sensually. "Now will you come here? Or shall I come to you?"

Caroline gazed at him in frustration. "Luis—it means Esteban was depriving you of something that was rightfully yours," she protested.

"But Esteban is dead," remarked Luis flatly. "And I have so much. How can I blame him now?"

Caroline sighed, but as his lazy fingers slid over her thigh from knee to hipbone, her protestations vanished beneath a tide of desire too strong to resist.

"But what about your mother?" she whispered finally, as his mouth sought the parted sweetness of hers. "Will you tell her?"

"I will tell her," agreed Luis half impatiently, silencing her further with a breath-stopping kiss. "But it will not make any difference to her. She is happy where she is. You know it. In that, as in all other things, Esteban was the loser."

"You're very generous," she breathed huskily, and his smile was triumphant.

"I can afford to be," he assured her softly, and sought possession of that which was undeniably his.

What the press says about Harlequin romance fiction...

Harlequin Presents...

The books that let you escape
into the wonderful world of romance!
Trips to exotic places... interesting
plots... meeting memorable people...
the excitement of love....These are
integral parts of Harlequin Presents—
the heartwarming novels read by
women everywhere.

Many early issues are now available.
Choose from this great selection!

Choose from this great selection of exciting Harlequin Presents editions

Relive a great romance...
with Harlequin Presents
Complete and mail this coupon today!

Harlequin Reader Service

In U.S.A.
MPO Box 707
Niagara Falls, N.Y. 14302

In Canada
649 Ontario St.
Stratford, Ontario, N5A 6W2

Please send me the following Harlequin Presents novels. I am enclosing my check or money order for $1.50 for each novel ordered, plus 59¢ to cover postage and handling.

☐ 99	☐ 103	☐ 109
☐ 100	☐ 106	☐ 110
☐ 101	☐ 107	☐ 111
☐ 102	☐ 108	☐ 112

Number of novels checked @ $1.50 each = $_____

N.Y. and Ariz. residents add appropriate sales tax. $_____

Postage and handling $_____ .59

TOTAL $_____

I enclose _____
(Please send check or money order. We cannot be responsible for cash sent through the mail.)

Prices subject to change without notice

NAME _____
(Please Print)

ADDRESS _____

CITY _____

STATE/PROV. _____

ZIP/POSTAL CODE _____

Offer expires December 31, 1981.   104563170